MIRROR, MIRROR

Read More by Andaleeb Wajid for Duckbill
When She Went Away

Read More for Young Adults from Duckbill
The Lies We Tell by Himanjali Sankar
Talking of Muskaan by Himanjali Sankar
Zombiestan by Mainak Dhar
Jobless Clueless Reckless by Revathi Suresh
Facebook Phantom by Suzanne Sangi
The Right Kind of Dog by Adil Jussawalla
Shiva and the Rise of the Shadows by Kanika Dhillon
The Wordkeepers by Jash Sen
Skyserpents by Jash Sen
Daddy Come Lately by Rupa Gulab
Unbroken by Nandhika Nambi
Invisible People by Harsh Mander
Wanting Mor by Rukhsana Khan
When Morning Comes by Arushi Raina
Year of the Weeds by Siddhartha Sarma
The Magicians of Madh by Aditi Krishnakumar
Murder in Melucha by Aditi Krishnakumar
Queen of Ice by Devika Rangachari
Queen of Earth by Devika Rangachari
Queen of Fire by Devika Rangachari

MIRROR, MIRROR

Andaleeb Wajid

An imprint of Penguin Random House

DUCKBILL BOOKS

USA | Canada | UK | Ireland | Australia
New Zealand | India | South Africa | China | Singapore

Duckbill Books is part of the Penguin Random House group of companies
whose addresses can be found at global.penguinrandomhouse.com

Published by Penguin Random House India Pvt. Ltd
4th Floor, Capital Tower 1, MG Road,
Gurugram 122 002, Haryana, India

First published in Duckbill Books by
Penguin Random House India 2021

ISBN 9780143451945

Typeset in Centaur by DiTech Publishing Services Pvt. Ltd

Printed at Manipal Technologies Limited, India

www.penguin.co.in

MIX
Paper | Supporting
responsible forestry
FSC® C043100

1

I thought my seventeenth birthday was going to be like any other. Boy, was I wrong.

My phone started beeping with birthday notifications from the moment it struck midnight, but I slept through it all. I even allowed myself to skip yoga in the morning and stay in bed for ten minutes longer than I usually did.

I glanced at my phone and saw that I had missed calls from my best friends, Nisha and Anirudh. We had holidays for Dasara in college, and had decided to meet at a cafe for lunch.

My parents had been subdued since morning. We had planned to go out for dinner, just the three of us. I should have known something was up when Papa agreed to my choice of the restaurant. He *hated* The Green Revolution. He insisted that grass is for cows and pooh-poohed my food choices all the time. But even that didn't tip me off.

During lunch with Nisha and Anirudh at the cafe, things were a bit weird and, at first, I couldn't figure out why. I observed the two of them and realized that they were not behaving as usual.

Anirudh looked troubled and Nisha seemed miserable. I suddenly realized what had happened. There was something going on between the two of them — something to do with their feelings for each other. Either Anirudh had said something to Nisha, or the other way around and it had made things awkward between them.

I tried and tried to get it out of them but they wouldn't tell me. They said that we'll talk the next day, after my birthday. I even blurted out what I was starting to suspect and going by Anirudh's blanched face, I knew I was on to something. Nisha just looked away, shaking her head.

The birthday just went downhill from there. I needed to speak to Nisha alone, but that made me feel guilty too.

Nisha and I had been friends since Class II and we had been inseparable. When Nisha opted for Kannada as her second language and I, Hindi, in Class V, I switched my second language and followed her right into her class, not worried about how I was going to study Kannada.

Then, Anirudh came along in Class VII. He was a typical bespectacled, shy boy who had a rather wicked sense of humour once you got to know him. He'd sprayed the back of our chemistry teacher's saree with ink once and all three of us got detention for that. Probably because we were sitting the closest to him and he looked much too innocent to do something of the sort on his own.

When we walked into the detention room, he was busy trying to capture a lizard using a plastic bag wrapped around his fist. I'd normally run miles away from such a person, but we somehow became good friends and we continued to be, right through our tenth and now in pre-university college.

A part of me was worried about what was going to happen after this. Anirudh was going to sit for competitive entrance exams and study to be a doctor, Nisha wanted to study architecture and I . . . I was still undecided.

I didn't really like the idea of them together. I'd be the third wheel, the 'kabab mein haddi' *all the time.* They'd want to meet up and spend time without me. And if we made plans to meet, they would either be waiting for me to come late or leave. Aaaargh.

Later that evening, as I dressed for dinner, I put the two of them firmly out of my mind and wore the new dress I'd bought for my birthday. I glanced at myself in the mirror quickly, bracing myself.

My arms were still chubby in spite of all the yoga, dieting and exercise. The churning in my stomach began as I wondered if I should wear some sort of a shrug to cover them up. Why did I think I could carry off a sleeveless dress? I'd need to diet for another ten years to have the kind of thin arms that I could show off.

I paced my room for a few minutes, itching to chew my fingernails. I could do it, I told myself sternly.

I could step out of this room and face the world with my chubby arms.

Thick ankles.
Round shoulders.
Ms Piggy.
Fat Ananya.

No, I couldn't.

I yanked the door of my wardrobe open and rummaged through my things. I found a white scarf, draped it around myself and walked out. The whispers in my head hadn't died down but they were a little less sibilant. I tried to push them to a corner of my mind as I walked outside.

Ma gave me a look, but didn't say anything. I should have realized then that something strange was going on.

It was only when I was halfway through my boring orange and spinach salad that I noticed that Papa fidgeting way too much. Ma kept looking at him uneasily. What was going on? I put my fork down, finally, and dabbed the corner of my lips with a napkin.

'What's the matter?' I asked.

Ma and Papa started and looked at each other once again. I had a terrible sort of premonition. Something was seriously wrong. Was one of them sick or dying or . . .

Ma mumbled something and my eyes widened. I must have misheard . . .

'What?' I choked out.

I took a sip of my spinach smoothie, the gross taste not even registering on my tongue when Ma repeated her words, looking at Papa sheepishly.

'I said I'm pregnant.'

The horrid smoothie went down the wrong pipe and I sputtered and gasped, my eyes watering. This can't be happening. I can't die on my birthday, right after listening to this awful news.

Papa got up and quickly delivered a few well-placed thumps on my back.

Ma looked at her untouched salad and ate a few bites. I realized she was avoiding my gaze. Papa also looked away, trying to pretend he was anywhere but here.

'You're pregnant,' I repeated.

Ma looked up and nodded.

'How on earth did that happen?' I asked.

At this, Ma couldn't control a smile. 'Well, you know, the usual way,' she said. Papa had the grace to turn red but he still couldn't bring himself to look at me.

'Yikes!' I got up from my seat. I had to get out of here.

'Where are you going?' Papa asked, worried.

'Restroom,' I muttered.

I walked away, looking straight ahead and reached the restroom. Thankfully, there was no one else there and I washed my hands perfunctorily because I needed something to do as I processed this information.

How could my parents do this to me? On my birthday! I turned around and walked right back outside and marched up to them.

'Why did you have to tell me today?' I asked Ma.

'I found out this morning, Ananya. I was shocked, yes, but I wanted to share this news with you . . .' she said.

I sat down on the chair with a thump. This baby was *already* stealing my thunder.

'We wanted to tell you later but your father felt we should tell you right away. Because you know, once I start getting morning sickness . . .'

'Stop,' I told her. I did not want to know more.

'Listen, love, this doesn't change a thing,' Ma said.

I refused to answer her. How could Ma think that this wouldn't change anything?

'It will be great, Ananya. Think of the fun we'll have!' she said.

Fun! Fun? I didn't know whether to laugh or cry. If this had happened ten years ago, I would have been happy to have a sibling. Of course, I would have eventually realized what attention-grabbing monsters babies are. My classmate Anisha had a baby sister when she was in Class IX and even though she pretended to be thrilled about it, I knew she was not only embarrassed, she was also horrified because her parents had transferred all their attention to the little snit. Her mother had even missed her Class X graduation ceremony because her sister had a fever.

'Can we leave?' I asked them.

Ma and Papa looked at each other and Papa gestured for the bill.

Later that night, when I was almost asleep, a sudden thought woke me up.

How would I tell Nisha and Anirudh about this? What would they think? Would they laugh at me?

And the worst realization — the one that I'd been trying to avoid — hit me then.

My parents still had sex. Yikes.

2

I was at Nisha's door the following morning, waiting for her to open it, when my phone rang.

'Ma, I'm fine. Just spending the day at Nisha's,' I told her as soon as I answered the phone.

'But . . .' she sounded doubtful.

I exhaled loudly. 'It's a bit too much for me to take right away, okay? I'll be back home this evening.'

'Okay,' she said and ended the call.

I looked at my phone for a few seconds and shook my head just as Nisha opened the door. She looked surprised to see me.

'What's up?' she asked as she let me in. I waved to her mother who was reading something.

I liked Nisha's room. It was simple, uncluttered and one could just sit down and talk. Both of us sat on the bed. I realized Nisha was being awkward.

'Listen, about yesterday,' she started, looking nervous.

'I'm waiting.' I wanted to hear her story before telling her about my sad life.

'Yeah, so . . . the thing is . . .' she looked away.

'Yes?' I prodded her.

'I've never thought of him that way. I mean, okay, maybe once or twice, when other girls would comment about how cute he looked with his geeky glasses, it would surprise me. And then I'd look at him and actually see what they saw and I'd feel awful for thinking of him like that,' she said in a rush.

'Then, the day before yesterday, he asked to meet me for coffee. I thought you would also be joining us.' She looked down.

Wow, this was getting into yuck territory but I kept nodding encouragingly.

'So I was surprised when you weren't there. He didn't say anything even after we ordered our coffee. He was just looking at me and I was beginning to feel weird. Then, he held my hand and told me that he really likes me.'

'Oh wow,' I said, because I was not sure how to react and this seemed polite.

Nisha sighed. 'Yeah, I was just shocked. I . . . I didn't know what to say,' she said.

'And then?' I prompted.

She looked at me and shook her head. 'It's just too confusing. We've grown up together and he's always been there for us. He's our best friend. I feel so awkward about all of this now. So, I just got up from there and came back home.'

'What? But . . .' I couldn't help but feel a little sorry for him now. He must have been so confused.

'I need time to think,' she said. I rolled my eyes. 'I told him that too. We haven't spoken since then. Then we met yesterday for lunch with you.'

'This is weird. But . . .' I trailed off. I wanted both of them to be happy. But I also wanted things to be as they were. I didn't want anything to change. That was not what was going to happen in my life.

'He keeps messaging me. Telling me that he's sorry,' she said.

'Why is he sorry? I want to whack him a bit for doing this. And both of you for keeping it from me,' I said.

She winced. 'I don't know why he's saying sorry. Probably because he went and changed things between us now,' she said. 'And I wanted to tell you but . . .'

I sighed. 'So what are you going to do?'

She shrugged. 'What do you think I should do?'

'I can't tell you that! It's your life!'

She looked exasperated. 'What if it wasn't Anirudh? What if it was some other guy from college? Wouldn't you tell me then?'

She was right. 'Look, things have changed between the two of you, whether or not you decide to do anything about it. So why not give it a try?'

'Really?' she looked somewhat relieved.

'Nisha, you don't need my permission, okay?' I joked.

'No, not permission, but . . .'

'Approval? Ugh, I don't know what to make of it. As long as the two of you don't do any smooching in front of me, I'll be fine.'

'Shut up!' She hit me with her pillow.

'What? I don't think I can take it. And after I tell you what my parents told me last night, you'll know why.'

Her brows furrowed. 'Why? What happened?'

I let out a big sigh. 'My mother is pregnant. She's having a baby.'

Nisha squealed. Totally not what I expected.

'Oh my god, how amazing!' she said, clasping her hands together.

'What? You're serious?'

'Of course! It's so cool. There's going to be a cute little baby to play with! I'm so excited for you!' she jumped up and down on the bed in her excitement.

'Aargh. Do you know how weird it would be for me to have a sibling *now*? When I'm *seventeen*? How could my parents do this to me?' I fumed.

'Err . . . it has nothing to do with you,' she reminded me wryly.

I sighed. 'Nisha, stop being an ass, please? My parents could have had a baby any time in all these years. But *now*? Ugh!'

'What exactly is ugh?' she asked.

I rolled my eyes. 'It's kinda gross, okay? They're my parents. I can't imagine them getting it on,' I shuddered.

Nisha winced. 'Then don't imagine it. Just think of that little sweet-smelling powder puff you're going to have at home soon!'

'Sweet smelling? Please. I'm pretty sure they're either demanding to be fed or they're crapping all the time.'

'When you have a little baby brother or sister, you're going to be amazed,' she said, looking sure of herself.

Her words were just making me angry. Why wasn't she being more understanding? I thought that she of all people would get it.

'I *hate* it when you start giving me a positive spin on everything,' I said furiously. There were times when her constant positivity made me angry because I just wanted to let off some steam.

'Yeah, but you love me anyway. Look, we're almost grown-ups. We'll be in college soon, we'll get jobs and move out eventually. It will be nice for your parents to have someone at home too, right?'

I listened in silence.

'They could have got a dog. That's what everyone else does!' I muttered after a while.

Nisha cocked her head and looked at me, also in silence, so I felt compelled to add more.

'They're not *that* old,' I said, not particularly thrilled about the thought of my parents being lonely.

'See? Exactly. That's why they can have another baby now. It's okay,' she said.

I rubbed the back of my neck vigorously. What she said made sense even though I didn't want it to.

3

I felt a little guilty about the way I had been treating Ma so I went looking for her. When I didn't find her at home, I called her phone.

'I'm back home. Where are you?' I asked.

'I left you messages. You didn't see?' Her voice was a little muffled. Where was she?

'No. Why? Where are you?'

'At the gynaecologist,' she said. What? Already?

'But you just found out yesterday!'

'At my age, sweetie, you can't be too careful,' she said. 'Okay, I have to go now.' She hung up and I continued staring at my phone.

At her age?

Mom was just forty-three. But . . . having a baby at her age . . . I suddenly felt a spasm of fear. What if something went wrong and she died? All because of this stupid baby.

My throat closed with panic. I needed to talk to someone but didn't want to call up Nisha. Obviously, I didn't want to talk to Anirudh about it either. I called up Papa instead.

'What is it?' he asked, his voice coming muffled too.

'Are you also at the gynaecologist's?' I asked, surprised.

'Yes, of course,' he said gruffly. 'What is it, Ananya?'

'I . . .' I didn't know how to tell him what I'd been thinking.

'Nothing. I'll see you at home,' I said.

'Okay,' he said and he hung up too.

I sat on my bed, feeling out of sorts. I needed to do something. I needed to take my mind off this panic.

I rolled out my yoga mat and did a few stretches, and then sat down, trying to calm my mind. It wasn't working. My mind was fixated on something else. Something with chocolate in it.

No, we're not going there, I told my mind firmly.

Please?

One square of dark chocolate wouldn't hurt anyone. I knew Ma kept a stash in the fridge but I had never ventured near it, as though afraid it would bite me.

Saliva pooled under my tongue and I felt an unbearable urge to just taste one little piece.

No. I knew exactly how to change that. I got up from the yoga mat and, bracing myself, walked over to the mirror.

That one piece of chocolate is going to show on your tummy, I told myself, making myself study my reflection. On your thighs. Do you want that?

I pinched my stomach and winced at the pain. Despite all the crunches, this was never going to go away, was it?

Fat bitch. Ugly cow. You'll always be like this.

The thought of chocolate was no longer appealing. I sat in the hall, waiting for my parents to return home and when I heard the sound of the car, I got up to meet them at the door. I looked for an indication on Ma's face that everything was all right. But she looked fatigued and anxious.

'What is it? Are you going to die?' the words tripped out of my mouth before I realized how silly I sounded.

Ma sidestepped me and walked towards the living room slowly. Papa followed her, looking grim, holding on to a file.

I held his thick wrist and he stopped. 'What is it? You guys are scaring me,' I whispered to him.

He looked confused. 'Why are you scared? Everything is fine,' he said. I didn't believe him because his face looked drawn and worried.

'But?'

'But your mom needs to be really careful. A lot of women give birth in their forties but it just gets trickier with age and the doctor has advised her to rest as much as possible,' he said, walking towards the living room.

I followed them, my mind racing. I knew Nisha was right. I had to be supportive of my mother and not act like a child.

Ma was sitting on the sofa, looking into the distance as though lost in her own thoughts. Papa was also sitting silently, looking at his phone.

'You guys . . . why the long faces?' I asked them. Ma looked at me then.

'You don't know this, but . . .' she looked at Papa as though for support and he nodded, putting his phone aside.

'I got pregnant when you were twelve,' she said.

'What?' I sat down, my legs suddenly feeling shaky.

She nodded. 'I had a miscarriage when I was two months along,' she sighed. The words burned into my brain. This was five years ago . . . when my own life changed. How had I missed all this? Why hadn't they said anything to me?

She sighed. 'Because of that and my age, the doctor says I need to be really careful with this pregnancy,' she said, her fingers worrying the edge of her pallu.

I got up from the sofa, only to sit down next to her, wishing I could rewind to the time when I was foolishly young and clueless about everything.

'Okay. I'm here for you,' I told her, holding her hand.

'Thanks, love. But we're going to need a lot more help,' she said. I frowned.

'What do you mean?'

'I spoke to V on the way back from the gynaecologist. She's agreed to come and stay with us for a few months,' she said.

'Aunty V? But why?' I asked, my heart sinking as it always did whenever Ma mentioned her name.

'Because everyone else is too busy and I need help and support,' Ma said. I knew that it was not that Aunty V was not busy — it was just that she could work from anywhere as all the multiple freelance jobs she did — editing, writing — were all from home, which was why she would have no problem staying with us.

I wanted to get up from there and walk away. But I needed to support my parents, no matter how difficult it got for me.

But . . . Aunty V? I have nothing against Aunty V, really. It was her son who was the problem. But then, that was years and years ago and Ma had only mentioned Aunty V. There was no talk of Raghu yet.

I was not going to think of Raghu, with his crazy hair and his shining eyes and that chipped front tooth that he flashed whenever he smiled. I wasn't going to think of that strange hot and cold sensation that passed through my body when his name was mentioned. I was *not* going to think of him.

Aunty V was Ma's best friend in college. They remained close friends and Ma was the bridesmaid at Aunty V's wedding. When my parents got married, Aunty V took care of everything. There is an awful wedding video that my parents watch every other year on their anniversary and Aunty V is in it, wearing a ghastly blue ghagra, flitting about everywhere. Seriously, fashion in the 2000s sucked.

I looked at them as they continued sitting there. Ma was lying down on the sofa now while Papa looked at her anxiously. Maybe having Aunt V over would actually be a good thing. She'd definitely make my mother feel better and make her laugh.

Aunty V was an absolute riot and I thought she was very cool and unstuffy. Nothing like an adult. She was shorter than me and would always inform me primly that she was 'petite' whenever she noticed that even I was taller than her. Of course, it had been a couple of years since we had met. She had come from Mumbai on a fleeting visit to see some ailing relative and had come home for lunch.

I remember the visit well. I remember feeling conscious of her staring at my plate and how little there was on it but I prayed she wouldn't bring it up. She was too busy talking about Raghu and how much he annoyed her.

'Sometimes I think I'm going to kill him,' she'd announced.

'I'll help you hide his body,' I replied. At this, she and Ma both looked at me in surprise.

'Ananya!' Ma looked at me sternly.

'What?' I asked.

My history with Raghu was something they were not privy to, so I smiled to let them know I was joking. Aunty V was worried about Raghu not paying enough attention in school. He had his Class X exams and apparently, all he did was spend time in the kitchen, trying new recipes and learning how to cook. I'd hated him even more when I heard that.

I glanced at Ma now, really, really hoping he wasn't going to come with Aunty V.

'So how long will she be here?' I asked.

Ma looked up. 'Till the delivery obviously.'

What? The whole nine months?

I wish Ma could call Nani or anyone else. But Ma has always had a tense relationship with Nani. They never got along and arguing with Nani would only increase Ma's blood pressure. It was a really good thing that Nani didn't live in Bangalore, but in Chandigarh.

'Okay. I'm here if you need me for anything,' I told her, getting up.

I was tired and I wanted to go back to my room and not think of anything.

Maybe things wouldn't be so bad. I realized I had been so worried about Aunty V and Raghu that I had stopped worrying about the baby that was going to change our lives. I didn't know which was worse.

Ma and Papa were talking softly when I left. Once college began, I would get busy and it was a good thing if someone else was there for Ma, to be with her at home.

I lay down on the bed and opened Instagram. Despite knowing this was a bad idea, I looked up Raghu's profile. I frowned when I saw that his Instagram was private. Since I wasn't following him, I couldn't see anything. Even his profile picture didn't reveal much. It was him looking out at the setting sun and his face was in the shadows. I didn't send him a follow request.

I looked him up on Facebook then. Here, too, everything was private. And we obviously weren't friends. Why I was doing this to myself? After all, hadn't I blocked him on Facebook some years ago? I decided to push him out of my mind.

I texted Nisha with the new updates and she called me back immediately.

'This sucks,' I told her.

She was silent for a bit. 'I know. But he's not going to be around. Just focus on your mother,' she said finally.

I rolled my eyes. 'Yes, mom,' I told her.

'Listen, don't get worked up over nothing,' she told me. Sometimes, I really didn't know how she got to be so wise. Or did she just say these platitudes because they were easy?

'Fine,' I told her, exasperated.

'And . . . it was so many years ago, Ananya. Maybe you should just forgive him and move on,' she said, haltingly.

'I've moved on,' I told her tightly. 'And you're making it sound like he was my boyfriend.'

'No. But he *was* one of your best friends,' she reminded me gently.

'Whatever,' I told her and hung up.

I decided to take a nap to take my mind off everything. But my mind could not stop reliving my humiliation from five years ago.

4

Five years ago

I came back from school, washed up and went looking for Ma. Knowing that she was probably in the kitchen, I walked in and stopped short when I realized that she wasn't alone. She was busy talking to Aunty V as she made a sandwich. Aunty V was sniffling and saying something. I felt like I had interrupted something. They both turned to face me and Aunty V wiped her eyes and smiled at me.

'Hey Ananya! When did you come home?' she asked me. Her voice sounded shaky.

'Just now. But when did you come to Bangalore?' I asked her as I edged myself on to the chair near the kitchen island.

'This afternoon,' she replied, as Ma placed a plate of sandwiches before me. I took one and bit into it hungrily. Yum. Ma had shredded tandoori chicken

and mixed it with mayo and grated carrots for
the filling.

'Raghu!' Ma called out and I started.

'Raghu's here too?' I asked in surprised excitement.

Aunty V nodded and gave a strained smile. They
had to call him twice before he came, looking more
tanned than ever. He had cut his hair really short
and he'd grown taller. He waved at me before sitting
down at the table, looking sullen.

'Where were you?' Aunty V asked him.

He shrugged, pulled the plate of sandwiches
towards himself and started eating. I stared at him.
I always looked forward to Aunty V's visits because
of how much fun Raghu was. But he barely looked at
me now as he scarfed down the sandwiches. Aunty
V stared at him too, but didn't say anything and
turned away.

Ma and Aunty V were back near the sink, talking
in low tones, so I couldn't really hear anything.

'What's up?' I asked him.

He shook his head and then slightly inclined his
head to one side, indicating that I follow him. I got up
and together we walked out of the apartment, down
the flight of steps, past the other apartments, into the
garden and sat down at the swings.

'My parents are getting a divorce,' he said,
kicking his feet into the sand and pushing back so the
swing moved.

'What?'

He continued swinging back and forth, but didn't offer any more information.

'But why?' I persisted.

'No idea,' he replied finally. 'They had a huge fight and Mom said she needed time to think and then we came here.'

I didn't know what to say to that. I didn't really know his father because I had rarely met him over the years. Soon, the other kids from the apartment started coming into the park, as we continued swinging in silence.

'Do you mind?' Esha asked, arms folded across her chest.

I looked up at her, surprised. Mind what?

'If you're not going to use the swing . . .' she added impatiently.

'Oh, right.' I got down in such a hurry that I twisted my ankle and fell down in an ungainly manner. I was mortified.

Esha was new to the apartment complex and she was everything that I wasn't. I could stare at her for hours — she was perfect. We were apparently the same age but she looked like a model. She had straight hair, straight teeth and beautiful, big eyes.

I got up wincing, dusted my knees and limped away to make way for her.

Raghu slid down from his swing easily, unlike me. I waited for him to join me but he was staring at Esha.

She turned to him, propelling herself daintily with her feet. 'Hi, my name's Esha.'

'Raghu,' he replied.

Someone came and sat on the swing he had just vacated and Raghu and I moved away. But Raghu turned back to look at Esha, who was laughing as one of her friends pushed her high into the air. Her laughter was almost like music.

'Who's that?' he asked as we walked around the garden and sat down at one of the benches.

'New family in the building. They've been here for a couple of months,' I said.

He turned to me. 'I don't know what's going to happen if my parents get divorced,' he said, his attention focused on me once more.

I didn't know what to tell him. He looked sad and worried. I squeezed his hand lightly.

Evening came upon us suddenly and the lights in the garden switched on. From somewhere, I could hear Esha's tinkling laughter and I felt a weird sort of happy-sad feeling run through me. I was really happy Raghu was here. And sad because he was feeling sad.

'I learnt a new recipe! Peanut butter and chocolate chip cookies! Want to bake them with me?' I asked suddenly.

He turned to me and made a face.

'Oh come on. It will be fun.'

'Baking is for sissies,' he said, rolling his eyes.

'What nonsense! Who said that to you?' I asked, genuinely annoyed.

He looked away. 'Fine. I'm not going to actually do any of the baking though. I'm going to watch and eat the cookies as soon as they come out of the oven,' he said.

'We'll see,' I told him.

And, indeed, a couple of hours later, when Aunty V and Ma came to the kitchen for something, they stopped short.

'Who made this mess?' Ma asked sharply. The culprit was easy to discover. After all, Raghu was the one covered in flour and bits of egg. The idiot didn't know how to crack an egg and ended up crushing it in his fist because he held it too tightly. Before that, he had enthusiastically offered to sieve the flour, and most of it ended up on his t-shirt. For someone who hadn't been too keen on baking, there had been a light in his eyes that hadn't been there before. I think both Ma and Aunty V noticed it.

'We were just baking,' I explained, offering both of them warm cookies from the tray that I had pulled out from the oven.

Aunty V looked a bit dubious but her expression changed when she bit into it. All four of us ended up sitting at the kitchen island, eating the remaining cookies, licking melted peanut butter and chocolate from our fingers. It was good to see Raghu laugh and even Aunty V seemed to have momentarily forgotten her problems as she made plans to stay in Bangalore for the weekend with us.

I was excited at first because that meant Raghu would be around longer. Usually his visits were fleeting. Then I remembered the reason he was here in the first place and my face fell, but I rallied and made my own plans with him.

'Still think baking is for sissies?' I asked when he reached out and took another cookie.

He made a face and then smiled. 'Can we forget I said that and bake something else tomorrow?' he asked. I agreed happily.

When I returned from school the next day, Ma was in the living room with Aunty V and both of them looked at me rather annoyed.

'What happened?' I asked.

'Go and look in the kitchen,' Ma prompted.

I ran there and stopped when I saw Raghu, once again covered in flour. But he was humming something as he stood by the oven, waiting for the timer to go off.

'What are you doing?' I asked him and he turned to me in surprise.

'Oh hey! You're back! I wanted to surprise you,' he said.

'With what?'

'I looked up some recipes on YouTube and decided to try the simplest of them all,' he announced.

'But why are Ma and Aunty V sitting outside?'

He shrugged. I realized he must have asked them to stay away because knowing Ma, she would have wanted to interfere in everything.

'So how was school?' he asked.

'Good. The usual,' I replied. And then I noticed that the inside of the oven was smoking. My eyes grew round and I rushed past him and hit the main switch on top. He turned around in surprise.

'Oh . . . oh no! What happened?' he asked as I opened the oven door and a thick cloud of bitter black smoke emerged. The cake he had baked was charred and even the pan was ruined.

Ma and Aunty V came rushing inside the kitchen when they smelled the smoke.

After some checking, I realized that he had set the timer for too long and obviously, the cake had burned.

Raghu looked extremely shamefaced. 'I'm so sorry, Aunty Chitra,' he mumbled to Ma and then ran away from there without any further explanation.

I was exasperated and annoyed, but I ran after him. I found him sitting in my room, looking out of the window at the garden below us.

'Hey, these things happen. I burnt so many pans when I first started baking,' I told him, nudging his shoulder lightly.

He didn't reply.

I went to the bathroom to wash up. When I came out, he wasn't there. I looked around and then saw from the window that he was sitting on the swing in the park.

I went after him, but as I was about to reach, I stopped short. Esha was sitting on the swing next to his and they were talking softly. Seeing them together made me feel like an unwanted outsider.

I wanted to back away slowly and go upstairs, but Raghu looked up and smiled when he saw me. He seemed to be in a better mood already and he beckoned me to join them.

I walked up to them reluctantly.

'Esha's birthday party is this Sunday and she's just invited us,' he said.

I looked at Esha in surprise and she smiled back at me.

'Thank you,' I said, feeling thrilled that I was being invited to her birthday party. I'd never thought she would even notice me.

'Yes, please come,' she said. 'My parents will be sending out the invitations soon.'

Today was Thursday. I didn't have much time to pick up a nice gift for her. I'd have to ask Papa to take me out shopping, I thought.

I didn't know what to say to her so I merely nodded. She seemed so radiant and composed and I felt like a bungling fool in front of her. She was wearing dungarees with a white t-shirt inside and her hair was tied in a high ponytail. Raghu also seemed to be quite taken by her.

'Ma's calling you,' I blurted out suddenly to Raghu, who looked a bit stricken. I realized he didn't want me to talk about the mess he'd made in the kitchen in front of Esha. I nodded the slightest bit.

'Yeah, I'll come up soon. You carry on,' he said, almost dismissing me.

I turned around and walked back upstairs to our apartment, wondering why I was having all these odd feelings I couldn't understand.

5

Five years ago

Somehow, Sunday was upon us before I even knew it and I still hadn't managed to go out shopping with Papa for Esha's birthday gift.

Every day when I came back from school, Raghu would hardly let me finish my homework because he wanted to bake. After cleaning up the mess on that day, he promised Ma that he wouldn't do anything unsupervised, which meant I was his supervisor. But I didn't mind. Raghu was fun and we laughed so much as we made brownies and cake pops and cookies.

Raghu didn't talk about his parents to me again and I too didn't bring it up. But I had overheard my parents talking one night. Apparently, Aunty V and her husband were going to talk to a counsellor and then figure out what they wanted. My happiness for Raghu — his parents were at least trying — was also mixed with sadness over the fact that he would leave soon.

In fact, Raghu and Aunty V had decided to leave on Monday morning. It was good for me because I didn't want to go to Esha's party on my own.

Papa had gone out after breakfast and I didn't know when he would be back. I had hoped to have more time to decide on a gift for Esha but I was feeling panicky now. Raghu was useless.

'Gift? Oh right. I'll think about it,' he said and went back to playing a game on Aunty V's phone. Ugh.

I called up Nisha and asked for help. Nisha was surprised because I hadn't said anything about the party during school.

'I must have forgotten. Help me out! Please!' I said, clutching the receiver tightly. I couldn't possibly imagine what sort of gift a girl like Esha would like. She seemed so sophisticated for someone who had just turned thirteen.

The invitation had come from her parents like she'd promised and Ma had been surprised and delighted too. She always worried I didn't make friends easily and since I was close to Nisha and Anirudh, I didn't bother making new friends.

'Nisha! Help?' I reminded her.

'Um, I was thinking. It's not too late to get a book for her . . .'

'But what sort of book?' I interrupted her. 'I'll go mad trying to decide!'

'Okay, okay! How about you bake something and take it for her?'

I paused my frantic brain. Would something homemade be an acceptable gift?

'Why are you overthinking this so much? I'd think myself so lucky if I ever got your triple chocolate brownies as a birthday gift! I wouldn't share it with anyone!' Nisha said.

That clinched it. 'Aww. You should have told me before. I wouldn't have wasted money buying you anything!'

I hung up the phone and glanced at Raghu, wondering if I ought to enlist him, but he didn't really seem too bothered about the party. Funny, considering how engrossed he had seemed in talking to her on the swing that day.

Feeling better now that the decision was made, I headed to the kitchen where I told Ma that I was making triple chocolate brownies to take to Esha's house as a birthday gift. Ma thought it was a splendid idea.

I made two batches. By the time I had taken out the trays, cooled the brownies, drizzled melted white chocolate on top and cut them into neat squares, it was almost evening. I looked at the clock and yelped. Why hadn't anyone told me I was late? The party began at 6 p.m. and it was already 5 p.m.

I packed the brownies in the fancy light-blue cardboard box that I had bought at a baking accessories store, tied it with a fancier black satin ribbon with white polka dots and went to take a shower.

I wore jeans and a top. I looked at all my clothes in my wardrobe. Almost all of them were loose tees and jeans. Esha would probably be wearing a pretty dress — something I didn't own because I had never really thought of wearing anything like that before. I wondered if the next time we went shopping, I should buy something dressier. I shut my wardrobe door and went outside looking for Raghu.

'Oh, he left already,' Ma informed me. Aunty V was not at home. She had gone out to buy a few things to take back to Mumbai.

'He left for the party?' I was taken aback. I hadn't discussed it with him, but I assumed that we would go together.

Ma shrugged and went back to watching TV.

I picked up the box and then reached the door and stopped.

'Ma?'

'Yes, Ananya?' she asked, not looking away from the TV.

'Do I look nice?'

She turned to me and smiled. 'Of course. You always look nice!' she said.

Somehow, her words didn't make me feel better. I took a deep breath and left the apartment, deciding to take the lift downstairs. The party was in the clubhouse, adjacent to our building. I held on to the box lightly for fear of crushing the brownies but I actually wanted to clutch it to myself.

Loud music streamed out from the clubhouse and I walked up to the door, feeling anxious. It would have been so much better if Raghu had been with me. We'd have been chatting and laughing and I wouldn't have felt this nervous. I had a sudden fear that I would step inside and people would stop doing everything and look at me and then laugh.

That was silly, I told myself. The clubhouse door was open and I walked inside, pasting a smile on to my face. It was going to be fine.

The clubhouse had been decorated excessively for the party. There were streamers and balloons everywhere and the music system was loudly blaring some Bollywood song. I looked around, trying to spot familiar faces.

I wasn't too social with the other kids in the building and didn't go down to play with anyone. So I just knew their faces, not most of their names. I was glad no one had noticed me coming inside.

I looked around for Esha so I could give her the gift. She was standing by one of the tables, talking to someone else.

She looked amazing. She was wearing a long gown-like dress in pale yellow and her long shiny hair reached her waist. She was giggling with her friend Tara. Both girls turned slightly and Esha nodded towards her left.

Ah. Raghu was on one of the chairs in a corner, still busy with Aunty V's phone. They had been talking about him.

I walked to Esha and she turned to me, almost surprised that I had come. I was confused for a moment. Hadn't she invited me to the party too?

'Oh hi!' she said, smiling at me and I was relieved. I handed her the box and wished her.

'Thank you,' she replied softly, taking it from me and handing it to Tara, who kept it on a table where the gifts were piled up.

I felt vulnerable without the box with me and I almost wanted to take it back, hold on to it until it was time to leave the party. I had felt comfortable with the shape and texture of it in my hand and now . . . I looked around, wondering what I could do.

Esha's parents were busy supervising everything. I looked for a place to sit down although I wanted to go to Raghu and talk to him. He hadn't even noticed that I'd joined the party. I wanted that easy familiarity we had with each other in my home. Why had he come away on his own? And here too, he hadn't even smiled when he looked up and saw me. Was he . . . was he ashamed of being seen with me? What an absurd thought, I told myself as I found a place to sit.

I got quickly bored and wanted to leave, but I'd already seen Esha's father bring in the cake on a trolley. I thought it would be rude if I walked out, so I lingered, watching as Esha and her friends gathered around the trolley. She smiled beatifically as she daintily blew out the candles and cut the cake amid all the applause and singing. I too clapped and joined in singing.

I looked around for Raghu and found him standing to one side. He caught my eye and rolled his eyes. Then he inclined his head towards the door, indicating that we leave.

I frowned. What was wrong with him? The loud singing died down and soon everyone settled down to eat. I managed to find a spot next to him at one of the many tables that had been lined up.

'What happened?' I asked as I pushed my spoon into the soft raspberry-flavoured cake.

He shook his head. 'I'm just worried about my parents,' he said. 'I heard them fighting on the phone this morning too. What if this counselling doesn't work? What if they split up?'

I didn't know what to say to that. 'Just enjoy today. We'll think about it later,' I told him.

He looked annoyed. 'Easy for you to say that,' he muttered and got up and left, leaving the cake uneaten on his plate.

I eyed it, tempted. It would just go into the dustbin. Might as well stop it from being wasted.

I pulled the plate towards me and quickly ate it, only looking around after I was finished. To my horror, Esha had spotted what I had done and was staring at me. I smiled at her foolishly, hoping she would understand that I didn't want to waste food. She raised one eyebrow but didn't say anything.

I wanted to leave too, but Esha's father had organized a dance-off. Raghu had escaped all this and I was stuck.

I felt a hot flush of shame every time I made eye contact with Esha so I avoided looking at her. She looked bored and impatient, as though she was waiting for the party to get over.

Finally, when all the kids were leaving, Esha handed out the snazzy looking return gifts. She gave me two and said, 'Please give the one to Raghu.' I nodded and smiled.

I caught her whispering to Tara as I left, 'I hope she does give it to him and does not keep it for herself.'

My face turned red. That was a mean thing to say, I thought as I walked away.

Outside the clubhouse, I breathed freely and was about to head back upstairs, hoping to put the evening in a box titled 'we shall never think about this again' when I spotted Raghu walking towards me, a frown on his face.

'What happened?' I asked.

'I can't seem to find Mom's phone,' he said. 'I think I must have left it here.'

Before I could think of anything to say, he nodded. 'Come, let's go and look for it.'

What? Inside the clubhouse again?

'You go,' I told him.

'Come on! I need all the help I can get. My mother will kill me if I lose it,' he muttered, not even listening to me.

'Have you tried calling the number?' I asked, not wanting to follow him inside. He stopped and turned to look at me, exasperated.

'Of course. I only get the "not reachable" message,' he said.

The lights in the clubhouse switched off at that moment.

'Shit,' Raghu muttered under his breath. 'They're locking up already.'

'No. It's a power cut,' I said, pointing to the buildings that had all gone dark. The generator would begin humming any moment now.

'How are we going to look for the phone in the dark?' I asked him. I couldn't see his face but could sense him shrug.

'I don't want to take any chances. What if Esha's father locks up the clubhouse? Mom and I are headed back early tomorrow morning. She'll kill me if she knows I've misplaced her phone,' he said.

With strong feelings of misgiving, I followed him inside, hoping Esha and her friends had left and I wouldn't have to face anyone.

Inside, we couldn't tell if anyone was there. But we didn't want to make our presence felt either, so we both quietly looked under the tables, feeling around the space with our hands hoping to find it. The tables had been arranged against one side of the clubhouse wall.

I heard Esha's voice nearby.

'Did you see *how much* cake she ate?'

My throat felt tight. She was talking about me. Her voice sounded so sibilant and nasty I thought, as my breathing accelerated.

'Ya! When Aunty offered her another piece, she took it, even after taking what was on Raghu's plate!' another voice piped in. Tara.

I felt something hard and pointy lodge in my throat. I wanted to curl up and die. For a second, I was glad that the lights were off. Maybe I could slink away without anyone noticing. I was too embarrassed to wonder what Raghu must be thinking of this.

'Such a fat bitch,' Esha whispered loudly. My eyes widened.

'She has such thick ankles!' Tara said.

'I know! Has she even seen herself in the mirror?' Esha said.

'Ugly cow,' Tara chortled.

'Ms Piggy,' Esha added.

It was like a competition between them to rack up the most insults about me. I felt like I had stepped out of my body, listening to them. My scalp was tingling.

Esha's mother's querulous voice rang out. 'Esha, have you got all your presents? Let's leave!'

Please go, I prayed. I bent my head under the table and shut my eyes tightly.

'Yes, Mama!' Esha replied, her tone changing suddenly. Her voice came from nearby.

I wondered where Raghu was. Surely, he would have understood by now that they were talking about me. Or maybe not.

I heard the sound of footsteps leading away from the clubhouse and breathed a sigh of relief. But I was startled when the loud whispers continued.

'I think the ragpickers I've seen on the road wear better clothes,' Esha said.

I felt something weird happen to my face. It was turning hot and cold alternately.

'Ragpicker?' Tara whispered. 'Have you ever seen any *fat* ragpickers?'

'Oh my god, you're right!' Esha gurgled. 'Also, would you *believe* what she got me?'

'What?' Tara asked, breathlessly.

'*Homemade* brownies. Like . . . how cheap ya!' Esha said. 'My parents got such expensive return gifts for everyone and . . .'

I was holding both the gifts with me right now, even as I had searched for Raghu's phone.

'What did Raghu give you?' Tara asked.

Their voices had become slightly faint and I was relieved that they were leaving. Her parents had already left—those had to be the footsteps going away that I'd heard earlier. This nightmarish day could finally come to an end. I never wanted to think about Esha or remember that I'd hoped to be her friend.

I didn't hear what she said and in the midst of the confusion, embarrassment and shame, I wondered what Raghu had gifted her.

'I didn't even want to invite her for the party, you know. I just called her because I wanted Raghu to come,' Esha's words rang clearly, as though she was standing in front of me.

My heart sank as pity and shame combined in me.

Just then, the lights came back on.

6

Five years ago

For as long as I live, I would never forget that moment. The utter humiliation of being found under the table in the clubhouse.

Esha and Tara looked at me in surprised horror. Raghu was not under any of the tables but I could see him standing nearby.

I didn't want to see his face. I didn't want to see anyone's face. I just wanted to die. I was breathing heavily and I didn't think it could possibly get any worse than this.

But it did.

I tried to come out from under the table and then realized I couldn't because I was stuck.

It felt like time had slowed. I squeaked out to Raghu for help. He was frozen for a second before he bent to pull me out. My face turned red as I exerted myself, and tried to come out. To complete my humiliation, Esha and Tara joined in as well to pull me out. It felt like their fingers were digging into my flesh and I shrank away but there was no place to go.

My ungainly body, my shameful and disgusting body was defeating me every moment. Huffing loudly, I got out, scraping my shoulders and my back. My face was red as an overripe tomato that was about to burst any moment. Raghu's expression was blank.

I looked down, unwilling to meet anyone's gaze as I walked away, pretending I still had some dignity left.

Once I left the clubhouse, I ran and didn't stop until I reached my apartment. Only then did I see that I was still holding the return gifts in my hand.

I didn't want to talk to anyone but I had to give Raghu's gift to him. I couldn't face him. Not now.

Obviously, he was embarrassed to be my friend.

I walked straight into the guestroom where Aunty V and Raghu were staying. Aunty V was reading a book and looked at me surprised.

'Hey, what's up?'

'Nothing, Aunty V. This is Raghu's. He forgot it at the party,' I said quickly and I walked away. I was surprised I could talk normally. My throat felt like I had swallowed several pointy, sharp objects — raw and scraped — and it hurt to speak.

'Haan, but where is *he*?' she asked.

I shrugged and rushed to my room, shut the door and bolt it. My back hurt a little but I ignored the pain as Esha and Tara's voices floated back to me. Without thinking of what I was doing, I stripped down to my underwear and turned to the mirror to look at myself. My mouth dropped open in shock when I realized that Esha and Tara had been right.

I looked disgusting.

These rolls of fat on my stomach, my chubby arms, my thick ankles. Even my neck was fat, I thought. Dismay grew sharply inside me as I saw myself for the first time as others saw me. No wonder they had said those mean things.

Until this moment, I had never been seriously bothered that I was fat. I loved food and I loved to eat, and my parents had never stopped me from eating what I wanted. In school, I had heard the odd joke now and then, calling me 'fatso' or 'moti' and although the words hurt me, it had been for a passing moment and I had let them bounce off me.

I couldn't look at myself in the mirror any longer. Taking a deep breath, I walked away and sat down on the bed, still in my underwear. I hated my body. I pinched my rubbery thighs, my non-existent waist and looked down at the fat hanging from my arms. I was truly disgusting. I deserved to be laughed at. Everything that Esha and Tara had said about me was true.

Fat bitch.
Ugly cow.
Ms Piggy.

I was not just Ananya Kapoor any longer. I was Fat Ananya. This was how people probably referred to me. My fatness eclipsed everything else about me. It wasn't like I was very talented to begin with. The only thing I was good at was . . . baking.

Breathing heavily, I got off the bed and wore my clothes quietly. Baking cookies and cakes and eating them as they emerged warm from the oven was my favourite thing to do. And that was the reason I was like this.

How could my parents have let this happen? Shouldn't they have warned me, told me to watch my weight? Shouldn't they have been concerned that each day I was growing bigger, my tummy was getting larger?

How could they even bear to look at me?

How could they love me?

My throat felt tight with unshed tears. Food was my enemy. My body was my enemy. Hate, strong and fast, built up inside me, forcing out all other thoughts from my head. Esha had assessed me correctly but she was still mean, I decided. Her only motivation for inviting me to the party had been to get Raghu to come. My face blanched when I thought of Raghu hearing them speak about me like that and, of course, the disastrous moment when he had pulled me out.

Did Nisha also think this way about me? I wanted to talk to her honestly, ask her frank opinion, because I needed to know. She was my friend and she wouldn't lie to me. But I didn't want to talk to her on the phone and I would have to wait till I met her in school.

Anirudh was my friend too, but I wasn't yet comfortable asking him this.

My stomach growled. I was hungry.

I felt a sense of despair loom up inside me. How was I going to do this if I couldn't stay hungry for even an hour? We had only just eaten cake and snacks at the party and already my stomach wanted more. I pressed my fist to my stomach to stop the growling when a knock on the door startled me.

'Who is it?' I asked, my voice hoarse.

I would have to open the door if it was Ma. She would want to know why I had locked my bedroom door. But it was Raghu.

I could hear his muffled voice from outside. My face became hot once more. Shame didn't let up easily. My back felt prickly and I wanted to curl up in a corner of the bed and never get up.

'What?' I asked, unwilling to even go near the door.

'Open the door, no?' he said. I turned away, pressing my face to the cold wall. Raghu could have said something in the clubhouse. He could have told Esha off for being mean to his friend. I felt the tears come, hot and angry, and I swiped them off from my face.

'I'm tired, Raghu. I want to sleep,' I called out.

'Listen. I'm leaving tomorrow morning,' he said.

My lower lip trembled, but I couldn't think of anything to say. He had seen me at my worst and I didn't know if we could be friends after that. I thought of the plans I had made for the two of us. After we came back from the party, Raghu and I would maybe try making lasagne. I'd printed out a recipe from a website this morning.

'Okay, bye,' I told him instead.

I didn't hear his voice after that. I burrowed deeper under the bed covers, pushing my fist into my eyes, trying to stop the flood of tears. Something had to change and I knew it had to be me.

I didn't know how, but I had to do something. If I couldn't bear to look at myself, how could others?

7

Five years ago

In the days after Esha's birthday, I was scared of bumping into her in the lift or the basement. I stopped going to the park and I was glad Raghu didn't live in Bangalore.

Nisha was horrified when I told her everything the day after Esha's party.

'I think I can easily say it was the worst day of my life,' I told her. I was dying to ask her something, but was afraid of what she'd say.

'I can't imagine! What awful girls to say such things!'

'Do you think she's right?' I burst out.

Her brow furrowed. 'What?'

The words were physical objects in my mouth — hot and sharp. 'Do you think she's right about me being fat and disgusting. I know I'm fat and . . .'

'No!' Nisha said immediately, shaking her head. 'No.'

I felt a moment's relief but doubt came plaguing me again. Nisha was my best friend. She would never say anything to hurt me, even if it was the truth. Which meant that she was not the best person to ask this question. I covered my face with my hands, shaking my head.

'Listen, what she said was awful. You are fat but you're not disgusting. Why would you be?' Nisha reassured me.

Even if she had been lying, it felt good to hear it.

Some months later, I heard that Raghu's parents got divorced. I felt bad for him. But things had changed between us, and when he and Aunty V came to visit some days later, I couldn't look at him without remembering that moment under the table. I did my best to avoid him and I counted the days until he would leave so my life could go back to normal.

Our parents didn't notice — they were too obsessed with what was happening in their own lives, whatever it was. Only in hindsight, I now realize that it was probably the time Ma had that miscarriage. Aunty V had probably come to help out Ma then. I had been as clueless about their lives as they had been clueless about the upheaval in mine.

What soured Raghu and my friendship beyond repair was that I discovered he and Esha had started dating.

One day, the lift was not working. As I climbed the stairs, I heard Esha giggling to Tara in the stairwell about how Raghu had sought her out and had asked if she would be his girlfriend. The echoes in the stairwell made their whispers audible.

It was a moment of pure horror, as great as the one in the clubhouse.

'But doesn't he live in Mumbai?' Tara whispered.

'So what?' Esha asked defiantly.

'And what about Ananya?' she asked.

'Who? Ms Piggy? Fat Ananya's got nothing to do with this,' Esha's laughter tinkled.

Surprised to find tears running down my face, I swiped at them hurriedly. I ran into the nearest corridor as I heard the voices drawing closer, hoping I wouldn't bump into them. I felt betrayed by Raghu. True, we hadn't talked since that day but I had known him for years now. He had been my friend for such a long time. Raghu could no longer be my friend if he was her boyfriend.

I tortured myself several times, wondering how much they probably laughed at my expense, until Raghu's betrayal became bigger than Esha's meanness. The only way I could deal with all this was by painting him the villain and it helped me to direct my anger towards him. And since then, Raghu had no been longer a part of my life.

The present day

Even though Ma's room was far away, I could hear her retching in her bathroom. I winced.

Ma opened the door of the bathroom and emerged, looking pale and drawn. There were hollows under her eyes and her hair stuck to the sides of her face in sweaty strands. This stupid baby, I thought, irritated and suddenly anxious. Making Ma's life miserable already.

'Ma, should I get you some . . .' I read from my phone and looked up, 'some toast and weak tea?'

Papa grunted. 'I'll be glad if *someone* gets me tea,' he muttered.

Ma ignored him. She looked at me and frowned. 'Are you wearing perfume?' she asked, breathing heavily through her mouth.

'Yes?'

Ma swivelled and went back inside the bathroom, retching, before I could say anything else.

I'd fallen asleep to memories I had blocked from my head for years. When I opened my eyes, I was surprised to find myself in this bedroom. I almost expected to be in the apartment where we had lived five years ago.

I shook my head. It was useless thinking about the past, but it was lodged firmly in my head.

I took a quick shower and wiped my body dry, my thoughts still with the Ananya of five years ago. As I dressed quickly, I looked at my body in the mirror briefly, half expecting to see the old version of me.

It was a relief that I was no longer that person. But I knew that I was still a work in progress. I was nowhere as thin as I wanted to be. With the dieting and strict exercise and yoga regimen, I had managed to nudge ten kilos off my body. I think if I could lose another ten kilos, I would be fine. Not perfect, but I might be happy with my body finally. I wondered what that would feel like. To actually look into a mirror without flinching.

I blew out a breath and googled 'morning sickn⟨ on my phone as I went to my parents' bedroom an⟨ knocked on the door.

Papa opened the door warily. He looked tired ⟨ very annoyed.

'What is it?' he growled.

'How's Ma?' I asked as I pushed past him into room. Ma was still in the bathroom, retching.

He raised his eyebrows in her direction and shrugged.

8

Despite my reluctance to accept this humongous change in our lives, I had to face it.

Ma had taken leave from work indefinitely because the doctor had told her she needed rest. Papa was worried all the time and I could sense there was some guilt too. My Dasara vacations were spent taking care of her, and making sure she was resting as much as she could.

She couldn't cook because the smell of the spices made her nauseous and she wasn't supposed to be on her feet too long. Since I refused to cook anything, Papa was beginning to get frustrated.

'No more Swiggy,' he burst out one day when he saw that I had ordered ghee rice and butter chicken for him. Again.

I glared at him. Poor Ma here wasn't even able to keep down anything she was eating and he was grumbling about eating restaurant food.

'V is coming next week,' Ma said. 'Can you just hold on till then?'

I looked away, hoping my face wouldn't reveal anything. Next week? So soon?

'I'm going to ask her to make that custard flan she does . . . her prawn balchao and . . . and her mutton biryani,' Papa said dreamily.

'Why are you having cravings when I'm the one who's pregnant?' Ma snapped at him.

He ignored her. 'Dal gosht,' he whispered dreamily.

I wanted to hit him over the head with something.

'Nihari,' he went on.

I slapped my forehead dramatically. Ma, who was sitting at the dining table, looked at me and whacked his wrist.

'V is coming here for me. Not as *your* cook, okay?' she told him.

Papa looked away sulkily and proceeded to empty the ghee rice from the takeaway container on to his plate and smother it all with the garishly red butter chicken.

Ma was picking at her food, just the rice and a salad I'd made for her with cucumber slices because that seemed to be the only thing she could eat without throwing up.

The night before college reopened, I was walking back to my room after drinking some water when I overheard them talking. Papa was telling her that they should have been more careful. Um. I wanted to get away from there as fast as possible—I didn't want to accidentally find out about their sex life.

But Ma said something that made me pause.

'I've wanted another baby, Shekhar,' she said. 'Ever since we lost that little one all those years ago, I've just had it somewhere inside in my head that I wanted another one.'

I walked to my room in silence, digesting this information. The childish part of me was annoyed that I wasn't enough for my parents. Why did they need another child? But another part of me was sad because my mother felt this way.

College reopened and I went from the drama at home . . . to the drama at college. Nisha and Anirudh had spoken to each other during the holidays. While I'd been busy figuring out my new situation, the two of them had got together.

They tried to text each other furtively in my presence and that made me feel like a third wheel instantly. I knew Nisha didn't want me to feel that way but there was nothing she could do about it. It was all new between them and I wanted them to explore it. I just wish it didn't have to be this way.

I often made excuses to go to the library so they would get some time together. I had probably never been to the library *this* much in my life. Phones were not allowed inside and I would sit at one of the tables and read a book quietly. On other days, I'd browse the coffee table books. I would find myself drawn to recipe books and despite myself, I would pull one or two out. I would flip the glossy pages and look at the beautiful photos, running my hand over the pictures, imagining how it would all taste. Just the thoughts were enough to make saliva pool at the back of my mouth and I would shut the books decisively and put them back.

I knew Nisha and Anirudh felt guilty but as I observed the two of them, I realized that this had been waiting to happen. The two of them had been attracted to each other even before either of them understood it. I had seen it way before Anirudh had told Nisha about his feelings. I had just refused to acknowledge it, hoping they would never act on it, because I would be left out if they did. Now that they were together, I was beginning to think of myself as an outsider both at home and in college.

One evening, I learnt that Aunty V was coming the next day. Ma had instructed Meena Akka to clean the guest room and make sure everything was perfect for her stay.

'Sometimes the size of this house almost makes me wish we were back in that poky apartment,' Ma said with a tired smile when I sat down with her.

'That apartment sucked,' I said without thinking.

Ma frowned. 'It wasn't that bad,' she said.

For you probably, I thought, but didn't say anything. Papa had always wanted to live in a house and when he could finally afford it, he bought this land and built this house the way he'd wanted to. While Ma seemed to miss friendly neighbours, I was delighted. No one should waste time talking to neighbours, I believed.

We had been living in this house for a little over three years now and I felt like I had come into my own. We even had a garden and it was all *ours*. It was perfect.

'Didn't you have all those friends there?' Ma asked, her forehead creasing. 'That girl Esha and . . .'

I wondered how parents could be so obtuse. 'I didn't have any friends there,' I told her and got up. Even if I had never told her about what had happened with Esha and Tara, it was just weird that she would think Esha had been my friend. She had never visited home and I had never been to hers.

I didn't want to think of perfect Esha and ruin the last evening I had with my parents before Aunty V came in like a whirlwind.

9

'**H**ow *much* you've grown!' Aunty V said, looking at me when I joined them after taking a shower on my return from college. She looked me up and down and smiled. 'You look nice.'

I frowned but I muttered a 'thanks' under my breath.

She cocked her head to study me but didn't say anything. I don't think she noticed the weight loss. It wasn't very obvious unless you were looking for it, unless I wore something form fitting or revealing. Even then, it wasn't like my body had changed in a life-altering way, it had changed over time. There was still fat that I was fighting all the time.

'At least her college isn't like ours was. They let them wear all this,' she said to Ma.

I raised my eyebrow. *All this* was jeans and a cropped top.

'Er, I'm studying in the same college you and Ma went to and if I ever went there wearing this, I'd be kicked out!' I told her.

'What?' she turned to Ma in mock outrage. 'Those idiots haven't changed the rules in more than two decades?'

Ma shook her head. They started talking about their 'good old' college days then. I tuned them out until Aunty V shrieked. I sat up on the sofa, startled. Even Papa came running to the living room from the bedroom.

'What happened? What happened?' he asked, looking at Ma in concern. He sat down beside her and then I realized that she and Aunty V were laughing!

'What's going on?' I asked Ma, annoyed. Aunty V's shriek was so sharp, it had most likely pierced my eardrum. Both of them were continued babbling, giggling and laughing until, finally, Ma controlled herself with a great deal of difficulty.

'I'm sorry! I'm sorry!' she said, and lapsed into giggles again.

I had never seen her like this. She was witty and said funny things all the time but I had never seen her laughing this much.

'No, I'm sorry. I shouldn't have yelled like that!' Aunty V said breathlessly. She wiped the tears from her eyes and then handed her phone to me.

It was open to the Facebook page of some middle-aged man. He looked serious and he was balding. He had a French beard *and* tufts of ear hair.

'Who's this?' I asked, handing the phone back to her.

Papa took the phone and frowned at it.

'This is Ashwin,' Ma said. Papa seemed to recognize the name.

'And?' I asked, still looking at the two of them in confusion. Ma actually blushed a little.

'Your mother had a crush on him for the longest time,' Papa said, rolling his eyes.

'Eww. That uncle?' I asked, dismayed.

'He didn't look like that in college,' Aunty V said with a smile.

'Oh, he was such a catch back then!' Ma said, almost dreamily.

Papa cleared his throat. 'I don't think so,' he said huffily.

'No, no, he was!' Aunty V assured us. She giggled. 'That's why, seeing how he turned out, I just couldn't believe it. And I screamed.'

'He was *such* a charmer but also a little annoying in the way he'd keep telling people to call him Ash,' Ma remembered.

'Facebook is amazing, no?' Aunty V asked. 'Imagine reconnecting with everyone from back then? You know what we should do? Organize a college reunion! A reunion party!' she clapped her hands.

Ugh. Facebook really *was* for Ma's generation, I thought.

'Err, Chitra needs to rest, V. In case you've forgotten?' Papa reminded her.

Aunty V's face fell for the barest of seconds before she recovered and smiled slyly. 'Of course. *You'd* know better. You're the one who got her in this state,' she remarked.

Aaaa! I got up from there, excusing myself and went to my room before I could hear any more.

Much later, when I stepped out of my room, my nose quivered. Something was wrong. There was such a delicious aroma in the air that my stomach grumbled loudly. I followed my nose all the way to the kitchen where I saw Aunty V leaning over the stove and stirring something in a pot.

She saw me and smiled. 'Come and stir this for me no?' she requested.

I didn't want to ask what she was making, but she announced it the moment I took the ladle from her.

'Your father says he's dying for my mutton biryani,' she said. I stiffened, but didn't respond.

As I stirred the masalas with the sliced onions and mutton, the rich aromas almost made me faint with hunger. I focused on finishing the task, but couldn't take it longer than a few minutes.

'I have an assignment to finish,' I said and handed the ladle back to her. I caught Aunty V's fleeting look of confusion as I walked past her.

'Okay! Dinner will be ready by eight!' Aunty V called out.

I went inside my room and shut the door, trying to get rid of the biryani smell from my nostrils. It was so hard.

I dialled Nisha's number and told her about the weird reunion they were planning. 'They're talking about having a party to reconnect with all these uncles and aunties!' I whispered.

Nisha giggled. 'My mother also gets excited when she finds someone she knew a long time ago on Facebook.'

My stomach rumbled again and I straightened up. My head was swimming with the temptation of the food outside.

'So Aunty V's making biryani,' I said casually.

There was a swift intake of breath. 'And?' Nisha asked.

'And nothing,' I told her. More than anyone else, more than my parents, she knew of my struggle with food.

'Ananya, nothing will happen if you eat biryani once,' she said in a carefully neutral manner.

Yeah, right, I thought. There was knocking on the door.

'I have to go,' I said, relieved and ended the call.

I opened the door. Aunty V stood there, hands on her hips.

'I told you dinner would be ready by eight,' she said.

'I'm not hungry,' I lied. My stomach chose to growl loudly at that moment. I didn't look down.

Aunty V shook her head. 'Come on, Ananya,' she said. 'A little biryani won't do anything to your figure.'

I felt heat rush up to my cheeks at her words because there was something patronizing about her tone. Was she expecting me to ask her 'what figure'? Or was she poking fun at mine? I kept quiet.

'What?' she asked.

I shook my head and told her I'd join them in a bit. Aunty V gave me a look. I let out a sigh.

In the days after Esha's birthday, I had started starving myself, punishing my body for humiliating me. My parents didn't notice anything because to all outward appearances, I was continuing to eat normally. It was just that they were too preoccupied to notice that I never filled my plate, and I always got up before them, so I could quickly scrape the food into the bin.

This took its toll when I fainted one day after getting back from school.

Ma and Papa didn't know the reason when they rushed me to the hospital, where I was put on IV. But the doctor understood that something was wrong and referred me to the psychiatrist.

Even then, my parents didn't figure out that there was anything wrong. I did not look anorexic. *Ha ha. I wish*, I used to think. I did not have bulimia. I wouldn't have been able to hide that from my parents. Of course, it was also because I couldn't imagine forcing myself to throw up.

The psychiatrist was a kindly middle-aged woman who asked me all sorts of questions, which suggested she figured out what was wrong. But I refused to go back to her. I didn't want to talk to someone who might want to make me to stop hating my body. Because hate kept my anger alive. Hate made me remember those words that were seared into my memory, words that still had the power to hurt me immensely.

Fat Ananya.
Ugly cow.
Thick ankles.
Ms Piggy.

Hating my body was the only way I could stop hearing those words from others ever again.

My parents didn't push me to keep meeting the psychiatrist because I convinced them I was fine. I just became more careful at making sure I wouldn't faint again. So, instead of starving myself, I became obsessed with healthy eating, exercise and yoga. The kilos didn't melt away magically and getting on the scale every morning was still a painful thing to do. But I had kept my love of food at bay and I was on my way to becoming the Ananya I wanted to be.

'Work in progress,' I muttered under my breath softly.

Aunty V, who was still waiting for me, cocked her head. 'What?'

I shook my head, not wanting to get into it.

I followed Aunty V out of my room but didn't go to the dining room. I went to the kitchen and quickly put together a salad, taking the bowl with me to the dining room. The aroma of the biryani wafted in the air and made me feel sick with hunger.

Papa looked animated as he wolfed down the food and Ma talked to Aunty V as they ate. I was glad no one was paying me any attention.

Then, before I could say anything, Aunty V leaned across and spooned some biryani on to my plate. I stared at the rice grains that were beautifully separate and not clumpy as they sometimes were when Ma made biryani. Not that I had tasted any recently.

I continued eating my salad and as I listened, I realized that they were talking about Raghu.

'I need him to get serious now, Chitra. This can't go on,' Aunty V was saying.

'Yes, but aren't you being too hard on him?' Ma asked her. 'He's just eighteen!'

'Yes, and he's already losing a year because of this . . .' Aunty V waved her hands around angrily.

'It's all right if he wants to take some time to figure out what he wants,' Ma told her gently.

'That's easy for you to say! Ananya is a good student. Not Raghu. I know that if he doesn't do these entrance exams, he'll just give up on studying.'

'Why? What does he want to do?' I asked, breaking into their tense conversation.

Aunty V sighed dramatically. 'He wants to become a chef,' she said.

I frowned. What, really? 'Does he know how difficult it is to make it as a chef? It's extremely competitive, the work hours are crazy and he's going to have to work his ass off for years,' I blurted out.

Papa cleared his throat. 'Ahem. Ananya. Language,' he said gruffly.

What? Oh, because I said 'ass'? I rolled my eyes.

'Exactly,' Aunty V interjected as though Papa hadn't spoken at all. 'I want him to go abroad. Study in the UK preferably. But this idiot boy . . .'

'The more you keep him away from what he wants, the more he'll want it,' Ma said.

I turned to her, surprised.

'Let him do it and see how it goes. If it doesn't work out, he can do the entrance exams.'

'That's what I've been doing,' Aunty V said in exasperation. 'Why do you think I haven't already sent him out of the country after his twelfth board exams? This academic year is gone.'

Ma was silent. So was I. Raghu was *this* serious about cooking? Since when? I felt like I hardly knew him—the boy who'd thought baking was for sissies.

'He wants to become an apprentice at a restaurant and learn from a chef. I'll settle for him getting an undergraduate degree at least. I've no idea what to do with him,' Aunty V continued.

Unthinkingly, my hand went to my plate of biryani. I took a spoonful and put it in my mouth before I realized what I was doing. The flavours exploded on my tongue and my eyes went wide.

'This is *so* good,' I said and Aunty V looked at me and smiled. I dropped the spoon back on the plate and got up. I had to leave before I ate any more.

'Where are you going? Not eating more?' she asked.

I didn't answer. Ma frowned at the food I'd left on the plate but I knew that if I gave in, I would have to atone later.

Raghu was still weighing on Aunty V's mind. 'I was wondering if Raghu said anything to you, Ananya,' Aunty V asked.

I paused by the door, my heart racing, my palms feeling clammy on hearing his name and mine together.

'Um, no. I haven't been in touch with him for a while now,' I said.

'Really? I used to think you two were close friends once,' she remarked.

'That was a long time ago, Aunty V,' I said softly and walked away. I marvelled at how clueless our parents could be. And yet, they were in charge of our lives. How unfair was that?

10

Ma's morning sickness woke me up once more.
I washed up and went to her room with the weak
tea and crackers that I had read would be good for her.

To my surprise, I saw that the door was ajar.
Aunty V was inside with Ma.

As I went in, Papa left the room to make coffee for
himself. I followed him to the kitchen and glared
at him.

'What?' he asked almost belligerently.

I was feeling irritated, but didn't know how to
articulate why I was feeling that way. I thought of a
lot of things I wanted to tell him, primarily having to
do with getting her pregnant and realized that this
wasn't a conversation I could actually have with my
father. Yuck, no.

'You need to support her more!' I said finally.

'What do you mean?' he asked, scratching his unshaven cheek.

'You can't just escape with that embarrassed look on your face every time she's feeling sick,' I said. And because I didn't want to see the said embarrassed look, I turned around and walked away before he could respond.

In their room, Ma was sitting on the bed, looking a little less pale. She was nibbling on something delicately.

'What's that?' I asked.

'Dry mango pieces,' Ma said. She seemed to be breathing out of her mouth, but was more or less in better condition.

'I keep a stock of them for motion sickness, but it's good for everything else too,' Aunty V said.

'Okay. Ma, I'm off to college,' I said, turning around when Aunty V stopped me.

'Since you didn't have much last night, I packed some biryani for you to take to college for lunch today,' she said.

'Um, no, I don't take food like that to college,' I told her, my face reddening in panic.

'How is it that I *never* see you eating proper food?' she asked, her hands on her hips.

I glanced at Ma, who looked up and frowned at me. I'd promised my parents that I'd stick to a healthy diet and not starve myself again. I may have lied a little bit.

I shrugged and made my escape, saying that I was getting late for college. I heaved a sigh of relief that the biryani didn't accompany me to torment me further.

We settled into a routine of sorts. Aunty V continued cooking up a storm. I tried my best to ignore it. It was not easy to open the fridge for salad ingredients and come face to face with a buttery looking caramel flan begging to be eaten.

Self-control was my mantra and I tried to focus on why I didn't eat sweets or rice or any form of carbs or fat. Fat. Yes, remember that, I told myself as I shut the fridge door decisively.

I often found Ma and Aunty V giggling over something. To my horror, I realized that Aunty V was serious about doing that reunion.

One Saturday, when I was at home, I heard them talking about it as I was coming downstairs after putting the laundry out to dry on the terrace.

'Any other time would have been all right. But now?' Ma said, shaking her head. 'I would be so embarrassed.'

'Of what?' Aunty V asked, looking genuinely confused.

'This. The pregnancy,' Ma said.

'But why should you be embarrassed?' Aunty V asked.

'Pregnant? At my age?' Ma asked, as though it was obvious.

'At what age? Forty-three? Please. That's hardly old,' Aunty V scoffed.

Ma was shaking her head vehemently. 'I have an almost adult daughter. To think that . . .' she covered her face in embarrassment. 'Everyone will laugh.'

'Who will laugh?' I rounded on her fiercely.

She looked up at me, surprised. 'Well, weren't you also embarrassed when we told you?' she asked.

I opened my mouth to say something and then shut it. It was true and I was still quite ugh-ed out by it and I did not want to ever think about how Ma got pregnant. But I couldn't bear the thought of anyone else treating Ma like that. It made me really mad.

'That's different,' I said finally.

'Anyway, the doc doesn't want me moving around too much until the first trimester is over,' Ma said to no one in particular.

'No problem. We'll figure this out once you're sorted and this baby is fine,' Aunty V said.

The baby! I sometimes forgot that there would be an actual baby at the end of this. I didn't want to start thinking of it as a sibling yet. It was quite mortifying to be honest. I was used to being the only child at home and now . . . I was no longer a child.

One morning, I walked into the kitchen before college to make myself breakfast and get an apple to carry for lunch and saw a pot full of cheesy looking pasta that made my mouth water. I glared at the offending pot and stalked away from it angrily, feeling awful for even enjoying its smell. I made a quick breakfast of an egg white omelette and some fruit but it didn't satisfy me the slightest bit. Not when the cheesy aroma still hung in the air and I was dying to have a taste. But I knew I wouldn't be able to stop at one bite.

In college, Nisha and Anirudh were too lost in themselves to notice my bad mood. We had a free period just before lunch and Nisha was smiling dreamily at Anirudh, who was explaining something related to organic chemistry to her, a subject that I hated.

I sat on the other side, getting angrier by the minute. My stomach felt like it had caved in and these two were being nauseating. I knew my resentment had no real reason except that I was probably hangry and I was taking it out on them. Not that they were even aware of it, I thought glumly.

Only when the bell rang for lunch did Nisha realize that there was something wrong because I was giving her monosyllabic answers. She knew I only did that whenever I was angry. I brushed off her concerns furiously.

'Why don't you just go and spend time with your boyfriend?' I snapped at her.

She glared at me and Anirudh winced. But the two of them dragged me to the cafeteria for lunch. I sat down sullenly, even more annoyed at the way my nose twitched at the many aromas here.

'Tell me what's wrong,' she said.

I stared at her and heaved a sigh. 'Everything,' I said.

Anirudh was toying with a paper napkin and he looked up at me. 'So talk to us,' he said.

'When do the two of you ever have time for me?' I snapped.

They looked at each other and I suddenly hated them in that moment, when they were a unit and I was on the outside.

'I asked you before . . .' Nisha began.

'Before hooking up with him?' I asked nastily.

'Ananya, you're not being fair,' Nisha said.

I knew it. I wanted to stop myself from saying hurtful things, but I couldn't.

'Yeah, you're one to talk,' I said cuttingly.

'Ananya, Nisha and I are together because we like each other. But you're my only other best friend. If you can't tell us what's wrong, how can we help you?' he asked.

I was about to tell him to take his help and shove it up his . . . when Nisha shook her head.

'This isn't you talking,' she said.

I frowned. 'What?'

'What did you eat today?' she asked me. She didn't wait for me to answer as she started counting things off on her fingers. 'Those disgusting crackers you always eat.'

'I had an omelette,' I defended myself. 'And an apple.' I'd eaten the apple in the auto to college because my stomach was churning from the smells of the cheesy pasta in the kitchen and it demanded more than the stupid omelette I'd eaten.

'Good. Then you can have something here,' she said and before I could realize it, she had ordered mushroom and cheese sandwiches for us.

I resolved to not to eat any when they came.

Anirudh was looking at me. 'So? Tell us what's put you in this bad mood?' he asked.

I blew out a breath. How could I put my weird thoughts into words? But I had to try because if my best friends didn't understand me, what hope would I have of anyone else getting me?

'It's everything. Aunty V is cooking up all sorts of things for my mother and father and they're enjoying her cooking. Far too much.' I could hear how resentful I sounded. I think that was one of my core problems. My parents were eating food like it was a normal thing to do while it was something I struggled with on a daily basis.

'And you're not . . .' Nisha trailed off. She knew about my struggles with food, though she didn't always understand it.

'Of course I'm not. I can't let myself enjoy food again,' I protested.

'But Ananya, if you eat something once in a while, it's all right,' she said.

'Says *you*. I can't take that chance again,' I snarled at her.

She sat back in silence and I could see her mind was working. But she didn't say anything. The boy who worked in the cafeteria brought over our sandwiches and kept them in front of us on the table.

'Why are you doing this?' I muttered to her as the boy left. My nostrils quivered.

Nisha knew my drill. She knew I ran miles away from carbs.

'One day, Ananya. If you eat something you enjoy just once, the sky won't fall on your head,' she insisted, pushing the plate towards me.

'You're my *friend*, Nisha. You're supposed to help me get through this. Not make it more difficult for me to stick to my diet!' I said.

She looked stricken, but shook her head determinedly. 'Never. I've never done that. I've always supported you,' she said.

Anirudh looked uncomfortable because it looked like we were fighting. We were not. I was just trying to get her to understand my point.

'Look, just have a little bit of the sandwich. Your energy is dipping. It's making you angry,' she insisted.

I looked at the plate. It felt like the sandwiches had little googly eyes that were calling out to me. *Commmmme*, they seemed to hiss at me.

Involuntarily, my hand reached out to the plate and broke off a tiny edge of the sandwich. I pinched the little edge and nearly brought it to my mouth, my body tensing in anticipation.

But good sense prevailed and I put it back on the plate. I'd already eaten a spoonful of biryani after years. I couldn't have a cheese sandwich now. I'd be giving my body the message that it was going to be getting more deliciousness and that wasn't happening. No way.

'I can't,' I said with a tight smile. 'I'll have a filter coffee. Without sugar.'

Nisha shook her head in disappointment. She picked up the sandwich and ate it.

11

A fter about two weeks, Aunty V needed to go back home for a few days because of some bank work she had to do in person.

It felt strange once she was gone. I missed coming back home to the sound of her booming voice. I didn't miss her in the kitchen though, where I could now go without fear of coming face to face with a caramel pudding or a pot of prawn vindaloo.

Ma was alone during the day when Papa was in office and I was in college. She looked pale and was losing weight! I worried about her endlessly and hurried home, instead of hanging out with Nisha and Anirudh as I usually did once classes were over. I always had this silly fear that something could happen to Ma. I messaged her throughout the day.

The three of us spent a quiet New Year's Eve together, sitting in the living room watching TV. I was wondering how much things were going to change in the next year. This was the last time we were going to be doing this, Ma, Papa and me. There was going to be a squalling infant with us in some months and next New Year, we would no longer be the same cosy unit.

I glanced at my parents, who were clearly not thinking about this at all. I was a bit resentful because my parents were already caught up with this baby and I was no longer their sole focus.

It was ironic, because all this while, I hadn't wanted them to focus on me. I hadn't wanted them to be on my case, asking which stream I wanted to pursue in college, or what I wanted to do. Now I was missing it because they were thinking of something else.

The following morning, I realized I could see the bulge under Ma's kurta. It horrified and fascinated me at the same time. Ma walked differently too—I noticed every little thing about her, despite not wanting to. She had to place one hand at her lower back. I used to think it was an exaggerated pose whenever I had seen pregnant women walk like that before. Ma told me that her lower back ached constantly and she *had* to walk that way.

Ma's bathroom breaks also became frequent.

'Pregnancies are so messy!' I told her one day and she burst out laughing.

'Why are you laughing?' I asked, surprised.

'You think pregnancy is messy? Wait till it's time to give birth. Then you'll know what messy is,' Ma said. I looked at her, horrified. I wasn't sure I wanted any details.

In February, the doctor said that Ma was now safe from any risk of a miscarriage, but she was still advised rest. Ma's face kept getting blotchy every now and then, and she looked tired because she couldn't sleep properly at nights. Stupid baby, I glowered at her stomach when she wasn't looking.

Ma's physical changes were quite acute. Her face suddenly became covered in zits and I couldn't understand why. 'It's the hormones,' she told me when I asked her.

And then her feet started swelling up!

My god. The number of changes that her body was going through! I couldn't take it all in at times.

One day, I was going to my room when I saw her sobbing in the living room. I rushed to her.

'What is it? Is something wrong?' I asked anxiously, sitting down next to her as she blew her nose into a hanky.

'Nothing.' Her voice quivered.

'Are you in pain?' I asked, not sure what I should do. I pulled out my phone, ready to call Papa when she shook her head.

'I was reading this book,' she said, handing me the paperback that she had been reading. 'It's just so sad.'

I looked at the book. It was *Confessions of a Shopaholic* by Sophie Kinsella.

I stroked her back and held her close. 'Shh. It's all right,' I assured her. She sniffled. I wondered how I had become her mom.

'Is it the hormones?' I repeated her oft-used refrain. She sniffled and nodded.

'What will make you feel better?' I asked her.

She shrugged.

'Should I make you some soup?'

She flinched. 'I'd rather die than eat broccoli soup,' she said.

'Ma! Don't say such things!' I said alarmed.

'Chocolate chip cookies?' I asked her. I could get some for her from the neighbourhood supermarket.

She brightened up. 'Yes, but I want them with a blob of peanut butter inside and I want a blob of Nutella on the top. And sprinkle some sea salt on top.'

'Huh?' I looked at her, horrified. 'I was going to *buy* you some . . .'

She shook her head. 'No! I don't want store-bought cookies.'

I took a deep breath and gritted my teeth. 'You know I don't bake anymore.'

'Yes, but your baby brother wants some.'

I stared at her. Was she serious?

'Brother? How do you know it's a boy?'

She shrugged. 'I just know it. When I was pregnant with you, everything was different. My skin glowed, my hair was so thick and beautiful. Look at me now.'

'Maybe it's because you're old now?' I said without thinking.

Ma looked at me and burst into tears again.

'Fine! Fine! I'll go bake some cookies!' I got up in a hurry.

I ran to the kitchen and then realized I had no clue about baking supplies anymore. I don't even know if we had any. The last time I had baked was when I had made those brownies for Esha. Not going there, not right now, I told my brain firmly.

I ran back to Ma and told her that I needed to get baking supplies. She was flipping channels on TV and looked absolutely fine. No sign of tears or sniffles. I rounded the sofa to see her.

'Ma, will you be okay if I go and get the things I need to bake the cookies?' I asked her.

'Of course,' she said, her eyes not moving from the TV.

'Ma? Are you okay now? Do you really need the cookies?' I persisted.

She looked at me squarely. 'You're asking me that? After what you just said to me?' I winced. 'Your brother *needs* the cookies, Ananya!' she said dramatically.

Aargh.

My baby brother (or sister) wasn't even born. And he (or she) was pure evil already.

12

I was heading to the store when the bell rang. I opened the door and felt my stomach swoop right down to the ground.

Standing before me was a much taller and leaner version of Raghu. What was he doing here? I stared at him, momentarily forgetting how to talk.

'Um, hi!' he said.

'Hi,' I replied weakly. That was when I saw the duffel bag resting near his feet.

Aunty V came huffing to the door and nearly walked into Raghu's back.

'Arrey! Why are you still at the door?' she asked him and looked at me. He stepped aside and she walked inside with a smile. 'Raghu, suitcase,' she reminded him.

Rolling his eyes, he walked out to the Uber idling outside the gate and lifted the suitcase that was in the boot.

Raghu was staying *here*? Had Ma known about this all along? Aunty V wouldn't just drop in with another person unannounced.

The problem was that they had no idea why I no longer talked to Raghu because they didn't know he and I weren't talking to each other any longer. She wouldn't have thought to tell me.

'Oh, you're still here,' Ma said, with a disappointed look on her face when I walked back inside the house. I had almost forgotten why I was heading outside in such a hurry.

'I . . .'

'Come, sit,' Aunty V beckoned.

I wanted to run away. I wanted to be anywhere but here. At the same time, I found my feet moving of their own volition towards the sofa where she was seated. I kept my gaze averted from Raghu, who was sitting near Ma.

I sat down next to her but before I could ask her about the 'surprise' visit, Ma sighed. 'My chocolate chip cookies, Ananya,' she reminded me.

I looked at her unhappily.

'Chitra, wait, okay? We just arrived. Let her take a breather,' Aunty V said.

'She's been breathing all this while,' Ma replied tartly.

I didn't know if Raghu was observing this exchange but I got up from there, angrily. 'I'll bake them,' I bit out the words. Even if it kills me, I thought.

'Good. I'm hungry.'

I stared back at Ma, wondering how she could make *me* bake. We had never talked about why I had stopped doing the things I loved. Why I had switched to a strict regimen of salads and why I flinched at the sight of anything with chocolate in it. Maybe if I had continued with the psychiatrist, things would have been different. I'd still be Fat Ananya, I reminded myself bitterly.

'Raghu, why don't you go with her?' Aunty V suggested.

'No need, Aunty V. You guys just arrived. You must be tired.' I almost tripped over their legs in my hurry to leave.

'Not at all. I'll come!' Raghu said, unfolding his long legs and getting up from there. I still couldn't bring myself to see his face so I walked away. I was going to pretend he wasn't with me.

We left the house and walked towards the baking supplies store that had opened up near my house recently. I did not look at him. I had seen the shop only in passing. I hadn't even been vaguely tempted to go inside. Five years ago, I would have squealed in delight at having a store like this so close to home.

Inside the store, familiar smells and sights assaulted my senses. Rows upon rows of chocolate slabs, packets of chocolate chips, jars of hazelnut paste and hundreds of cupcake liners. I was in heaven and hell at the same time.

I sensed Raghu beside me, reaching out to take something from a shelf.

'Don't you need this?' he asked, handing me a packet of demerara sugar.

'Yes.' I took it from his hand. His voice had changed—it was deeper and stronger. I was tempted to look at him but I kept moving down the aisle.

I picked up all the items I needed from memory, walked to the billing counter and paid for the purchases. Before I could take the bag from the shopkeeper, Raghu had taken it.

We turned towards the house, with me still pretending he was not there, though he matched his strides with mine.

'How have you been?' he asked.

'Good,' I replied.

'Ananya, aren't you ever going to look at me?' he asked, sounding almost puzzled.

I shrugged. It would hurt too much, I wanted to say.

'I don't know what you're saying,' I told him instead and continued walking doggedly.

He stepped in front of me and I almost walked into his solid chest.

I looked up at him finally, tried not to let the surprised pleasure become evident on my face on actually seeing him properly. At the door, I had been too shocked to look at him intently. He looked different and, yet, there were hints of the boy I'd known, the boy who had played with me.

'I just want to get home,' I told him, trying not to take in how his face had become leaner, how his shoulders had become broader. Or even the fact that he was so tall that I had to look up to see him. It was a bit like staring at the sun – disorienting and bright and with a feeling of warmth spreading through me that I didn't like. Liar, I chided myself.

'Okay, we're going home,' he said, stepping aside and we started walking back.

My mind crowded with many different things. Raghu had been like the brother I'd never had and yet, I could never really think of him as a brother. And those thoughts confused me as much now as they did then.

'It's been years since we had a proper chat,' he said, matching his steps with mine.

We walked up to my house. I put my hand out to push open the gate when Raghu's hand landed on my arm.

'Ananya, please,' he pleaded, his voice low.

'Please what?' I asked him, looking into his brown eyes that irritatingly reminded me of caramel.

He took a deep breath but before he could speak, I shook off his hand and walked inside the house.

My bout of self-righteous anger lasted until I reached the kitchen. Why was I angry with Raghu? Because he dated Esha four years ago? When we were kids? What did that mean to him? Not much, I surmised.

To be fair to him, he had tried to reach out to me a few times after his parents' divorce. He had contacted me on Facebook, but I swiftly blocked him. He had tried to reach out to me on Whatsapp but since I didn't have my own phone back then, he would message my mother and ask to speak to me and I would ignore his messages. He had given up trying and I had been sad at the friendship I had lost but relieved that I wouldn't have to see him again. Even after all these years, I would have liked to hold on to that anger, but in the face of his very physical charm, it was hard to remember why I had been angry with him.

I took the butter out of its cardboard box, weighed out the amount I needed and dropped it into a mixing bowl.

I had been angry because he had witnessed my humiliation back then and had tried to talk to me, but I had been too mortified to face him. Well, you can face him now, a voice in my head whispered. You're no longer the same person.

My jaw tightened. Anger helped me cope when I needed it. If I let go of it, I might do something stupid.

I measured out the demerara sugar into the bowl and started beating the butter and sugar together. Since the butter was still hard, bits of it flew out of the bowl.

I sensed a presence at the door. Raghu was standing there, arms crossed, looking at me in an infuriatingly amused manner.

'What?' I snapped, focusing once more on the butter.

'Um, I remember you teaching me that the butter had to be soft before you beat it,' he said, walking up to where I was standing.

I backed away the slightest bit. 'Yeah, I don't have time for that,' I muttered. 'Ma wants these cookies like yesterday.'

He was still standing near me and it made me feel weird inside. I shouldn't be feeling this way. This was Raghu, my childhood friend. But he was no longer that boy. And I was no longer that girl.

'What are you doing?' I asked him.

'Just getting things ready for you,' he replied, as he measured out the flour and sieved it into a bowl. He looked around for something.

'Cookie sheets?' he asked.

I didn't even know if we had any cookie sheets. I'd never used the oven in this house.

'Where are your baking supplies? I can't see anything,' he said, hunting through the shelves.

I stopped the electric beater and looked at him as he searched the kitchen.

'You'll have to ask Ma,' I told him.

He looked at me. There was a little flour in his hair. How did he always manage to get flour there, I wondered.

'Why don't you know?' he asked.

'I don't bake anymore,' I told him, switching on the beater once more and focusing on the butter and sugar.

'Then why are you baking cookies?' he asked, going back to his hunt. He finally unearthed an old cookie sheet from some shelf.

'For this stupid baby. Why else?' I muttered savagely.

He washed the pan efficiently and turned to look at me as he dried it with a cloth.

'*Stupid* baby?' he asked.

I clenched my teeth.

'Is that how you feel about the baby?' he persisted.

'Why? What does it matter to you?'

He looked taken aback at my vehemence. 'I thought you'd be thrilled to have a sibling.'

'Shows how little you know me,' I scoffed.

'True,' he admitted and went back to drying the cookie sheet.

I looked at his back and wished he would face me once more, so I could throw more accusations at his face. Boyfriend of my enemy. Witness to my humiliation. Things were building up inside me and

I knew I needed to defuse it or I'd say all sorts of things that I would regret later.

'Haven't you beaten that butter enough?' he asked quietly, still turned away from me.

'Yeah, I . . .'

He turned around and I realized too late what he was doing.

He broke an egg over my head.

I gasped in shock.

Egg dripped down the side of my face wetly, into my ears and I was scared to open my mouth in case I swallowed raw egg. Eggshells stuck to my cheek and slid down to my neck.

I didn't even think as I looked around for the nearest thing I could find — the flour he'd just sieved. I picked up the bowl and lobbed it at his head. He sputtered as the flour covered him.

We stared at each other in tense silence for what seemed like agonising minutes.

Then I began to smile. At the absurdity of the situation, the sticky yolk that was now running into my top and trickling down my body and Raghu looking like a complete goof.

He started laughing then and, try as much as I would, I couldn't control myself. I laughed as I hadn't in the longest time.

'I have to take a shower now, you fool,' I muttered when I managed to stop laughing.

'Take your time,' he said, coughing out the flour that had got into his lungs.

It was a wonder Ma and Aunty V hadn't heard the commotion!

I went to my room quickly and looked at myself in the mirror. Egg shells in my hair, yolk on my face and neck. Ugh. But even as I peeled my clothes away carefully, I couldn't stop myself from smiling.

13

When I emerged from my shower, I could still smell egg. I wanted to call Nisha quickly and tell her about the situation at home. But Ma wanted cookies and I had left the kitchen a mess. I didn't want Ma to stress over it.

I walked briskly towards the kitchen and stopped short.

The kitchen was clean—there was no sign of the mess we'd just made. Raghu was just pulling out the cookie sheet from the oven. What? He'd finished baking already?

He had dusted most of the flour off his face but there were some streaks in his hair that he'd missed.

'Idiot. Who asked you to bake them right away? Ma wanted . . .'

'With peanut butter inside and Nutella on top. I asked her,' he said, placing the cookie tray on the counter.

I could see the spirals of steam wafting from the top of the golden brown cookies that had spread beautifully. He took out the sea salt that I had bought and lightly sprinkled it over the cookies. The flecks of salt lodged into those pools of melted chocolate chips. My mouth watered.

He turned to me and smiled triumphantly. I decided to go back to the living room, now that there was no need for me to bake.

'Have one?' he offered, dusting his hands as he placed the next round of cookie dough balls on the sheet.

I shook my head. 'No, thanks.' I started to walk away.

'Ananya, wait!' he called out.

I stopped at the kitchen door.

'Um, Ma needs me,' I said.

'My mom is with her. Stay here for a bit, no? I thought we had stopped being weird around each other or do I need to break another egg over your head?' he joked.

The happy feeling that had been running through me dissipated. I was confused, but I didn't want to make a big deal out of anything.

'I just showered. And looks like you need to too,' I told him, pointing to the flour on his hair.

'Oh man, I keep forgetting to check my hair,' he muttered. 'I'll shower once I'm done.'

He picked up the cooled cookies from the sheet and put them on a plate. I marvelled at his efficiency and how quickly he'd cleaned the kitchen. When I mentioned it, he smiled.

'I still remember the dressing down I got from your Ma when I messed up her kitchen in that old apartment you used to live in.'

I rolled my eyes, my stomach clenching at the memory of those days.

Raghu continued working and I tried hard to ignore him. But he wasn't having any of that. He was constantly talking as his hands moved busily, and I found myself replying to his questions, finding that I couldn't stay annoyed with him. My anger had evaporated when I hadn't been focusing on holding on to it.

'My *mother*,' he said dramatically, shaking his head and picking up the plate of cookies, indicating that we should walk out, 'does not understand what I want to do with my life.'

I remembered Aunty V being upset about his plans. What irked me was that he had plans, while I had no clue what I was going to do.

I didn't respond and we walked to the living room where Ma and Aunty V were talking softly.

'I smell chocolate chip cookies!' Ma said, her face brightening and her eyes lighting up.

I rolled my eyes. She was behaving like she hadn't had cookies in a decade.

I sat down while Raghu handed the plate to my mother. Ma stuffed her face with one whole cookie in one giant mouthful. I watched her, bemused, as she licked the chocolate from her fingers. Aunty V and even Raghu laughed.

They both took a cookie each, and Ma took another one. When Raghu handed me the plate, I shook my head. 'I don't eat cookies,' I told him.

'Have one, Ananya! These are so delicious!' Ma proclaimed. 'I haven't had such delicious cookies in the longest time!'

I smiled tightly, but didn't respond. Raghu looked at me, as though seeing me for the first time since he had come home, but he didn't say anything.

I went to the kitchen to take out the next batch of cookies from the oven. Then I decided to spend as long as I possibly could in my room, away from Raghu and the delicious cookie smells.

I paced in my room for a bit, hoping that would help with the unease I was feeling. A lot of my feelings around what happened after Esha's birthday were tied up with Raghu and my anger at him. Now that had disappeared and I found myself thinking that I was had been incredibly silly. In fact, his goofiness a while ago had made me realize just how much fun he was.

I called up Nisha, who was very excited on hearing about Raghu visiting. She was behaving like he was *her* long lost friend, not mine.

'He did what?' she asked in a whisper.

'He broke an egg over my head,' I replied, fighting to wipe the grin off my face, which was kind of silly since she could not see my face.

'Oh man! He sounds like a riot. I really do want to meet him, Ananya. Let's hang out together this weekend, no? I'm sure Anirudh will be up for it too,' Nisha said.

'Hang out together?' I repeated faintly. What did she mean?

'We were planning to catch a movie. Come with him, no? Please. It will be such fun,' she said.

When I didn't respond, Nisha sighed. 'Should I talk to him and invite him?'

'No!' I replied. 'I'll tell him.'

'You have to come,' she said fervently. 'Please. Anyway, it's been such a long time since the three of us went out for a movie.'

I stopped myself from retorting that we hadn't gone out anywhere because the two of them were a couple and I didn't want to interrupt their time together. I'd already been mean to them about it once. There was no need to be bitchy again.

'Aniruddh's parents okay with him going for a movie?' I asked casually instead. Aniruddh barely had time these days, what with college and preparing for his entrance exams. He was going for coaching classes right after college and got back home only after eight.

'Yeah,' Nisha said softly. 'He's scared of the NEET exams and he wants to be done with it fast. He thinks life will get back to normal for him once he writes the exam.'

'Our finals are barely a few weeks away. In March! And you have to write the CET exam too,' I reminded her. I felt dread rise in my stomach.

'It's just *one* movie, Ananya,' Nisha snapped, irritated.

'Fine, fine. I'll come,' I told her. For all I knew, Raghu wouldn't be here for more than a week. Didn't he have to get back to his life in Mumbai?

There was a sharp knock on my door and I ended the call with Nisha.

I went to my door, knowing it was Raghu. I paused, took a deep breath and then opened the door.

There he was, a bright smile on his face—and oh god, why was he so tall?

'What?'

'Come out! Why did you go to your room? I'm bored!' he said. He'd apparently showered in the half hour I was inside my room and he looked squeaky clean and fresh. I still smelled of egg.

'I . . .'

Before I could make an excuse, he reached out and grabbed my hand. I felt breathless in a strange sort of way as I tried to pull my hand away.

'Okay, okay,' I protested.

His hand was firm and dry, and I could only focus on how strong his grip was.

I was having the most annoying reactions to him and I couldn't understand why. Or I didn't want to. Maybe it was because I had never really been close to that many boys, in fact, none except Aniruddh, who didn't count, of course. Since I was so obsessed with body image and self-esteem, I had never felt comfortable with anyone of the opposite sex or given much thought to the cute boys in college. Not that there were that many. Certainly not as cute as . . . Raghu.

He dragged me outside and I went reluctantly.

'Come on! My mom and yours are planning some ugh-sounding reunion with friends they have found on Facebook from twenty years ago. Did you have any idea about this?' he asked as he let go of my hand.

'Oh shit. Is Aunty V serious about that?' I asked finally. My hand actually throbbed a little. It could possibly be because he'd held it so hard, but I knew it was something else.

'Yeah, man. I sat with them for like ten minutes and realized that they want to actually do this the last weekend of February! I don't think I'll be around for that.'

'Why?' the words slipped out before I could stop myself. Idiot. *What do you care if he isn't here*, I berated myself.

'I guess I'll be back home by then,' he said.

As we neared the living room, I made a face. I didn't want to go back there.

'What?' he asked when he saw me hesitate.

'Nothing,' I said.

I could hear Papa's voice—he must have come back from work. It felt like my house was full of people—and I was still so alone inside.

'Hey, my friends want to go for a movie this weekend. Want to come along?' I blurted out.

His screwed his eyes shut and pretended to think about it deeply for a few seconds. I almost laughed at the face he made.

'Ya, sure! Why not?' he said.

Strange things were happening to my stomach. Raghu wasn't just cute. He was something else altogether.

14

We went out for dinner that night — all of us. Papa insisted on it because the doctor said Ma should move around a bit, but with caution.

He clapped Raghu on the back too hard a couple of times. Raghu grimaced at me, his eyes watering in pain. I smiled back. Ma locked the house and we piled into the car.

'When did this boy grow so tall, Veena?' Papa asked Aunty V.

'Uncle, can I drive?' Raghu asked with a hopeful look in his eyes.

Papa snorted but glanced over at Aunty V who shrugged. Papa looked at Ma, and then found the perfect excuse not to give his beloved car to Raghu to drive.

'Maybe next time? Since this is Chitra's first time out, we have to be careful while driving with her . . .

and you know how bad Bangalore's roads are,' Papa said slowly.

Raghu nodded in a good-natured manner but winked at me. I grinned back at him, realizing that in just a few hours, Raghu had made me laugh and grin a lot. I felt I could be free of my thoughts and all the things that bogged me down for at least one night.

I should have known that it wouldn't last.

At the restaurant, Raghu cocked his head just the slightest bit at me. 'You look different,' he said softly. Our parents didn't hear us and I was glad.

I smiled as I sat down, trying not to think too much about why I'd taken extra care with my appearance today—though I was wearing my usual jeans and a top. How I wished to be that final version of Ananya already—skinny, with thin arms and a thigh gap. I knew that the tyres around my body had reduced, and I was not fat, but what people like my father and well-meaning relatives fondly called 'healthy'. In my head though, I would always be Fat Ananya.

Though there was an empty chair next to his mother's, Raghu sat down opposite me.

He stared at me for a moment. 'It's been years since we actually spoke,' he said.

I looked down. Raghu quickly looked at my parents and his mother, who were busy studying the menu.

'What happened, Ananya? Why did you stop talking to me?' he asked in a low voice.

I looked at him and then away. The butterflies fluttering inside my stomach were not entirely because of panic.

'I don't know. I never really thought about it,' I lied.

'Oh, come on,' he continued in that low voice that was sliding under my skin strangely.

'What? Everyone gets busy, Raghu. You had your life in Mumbai, I had mine here.' I shrugged to emphasise my point.

'So you weren't mad at me?'

I frowned and picked up the menu, my heart thumping so loudly that I thought the whole restaurant must hear it.

'Why would I be mad at you?' I asked him, my gaze on the menu. *Everything* seemed fried here. Okay, not everything, but that's what it felt like anyway. The Only Place was one of Papa's favourite restaurants and we hadn't been here in a very long time.

I looked at Raghu over the menu. He was looking into the distance, lost in his thoughts. Before I could look away, he turned to me, snagging my gaze.

'I *kept* trying to reach out to you and you shut me down. You blocked me on Facebook,' he said, his voice a whisper.

Raghu had chosen a fine time to get confrontational, I thought, annoyed. He could have done this at home.

I smiled at him tightly. 'I have no clue what you're talking about.'

He made a face and turned to Ma suddenly, to ask her what she was planning to have.

Ma wrinkled her nose. 'Don't order any sizzlers,' she said suddenly, making a face as the waiter took a smoking tray to one of the other diners. 'That smell is awful.'

'Okay, okay,' Papa blustered. He looked around as though he was embarrassed of his pregnant wife.

Raghu and I shared a pointed look. He was trying to control a grin. I stared back at him, keeping a straight face. I kind of had a feeling both of us had the same thought running through our heads and it wasn't grossing me out to think of my parents doing whatever it was they'd done to reach this point in life. It was easier to think of it that way and not spell out the words S E X in my head.

I cleared my throat. 'I'll have the Greek salad,' I said, shutting the menu.

Papa rolled his eyes. 'What about you, Raghu?'

Raghu ordered a steak. Papa looked approving and turned to Ma and Aunty V.

'So that's what has changed about you then,' Raghu said.

'What?'

'You eat salads now,' he said.

'All the time,' Papa interjected.

I flushed. I didn't want them to dissect my eating choices at the table. If it were up to me, no one would notice what I ate or did and one day, I'd be magically thin and everyone would forget what I'd been like before. Ma and Papa had resigned themselves to my changed persona and eating habits because I had been careful about not overdoing anything. They just thought I had turned into a health freak.

'Let her be,' Aunty V said suddenly, and ordered a meatball pasta for herself. I hadn't expected support from Aunty V, but people surprise one all the time.

Ma, of course, stumped everyone with her order. She wanted everything on the dessert menu.

'But . . .' Papa looked at her in horror.

She shook her head firmly. 'Everything. And no one gets to taste anything from my plate. Get your own dessert.'

Papa looked at Aunty V for help but she shrugged. 'You did this, Shekhar,' she said, gravely. 'Now bear the consequences.' She burst out laughing and so did Ma, although Ma looked a little embarrassed.

'I can't bring myself to eat anything here,' she tried to explain. 'I only want desserts.'

'Fine, we'll get Aunty Chitra her desserts,' Raghu said, hailing the waiter.

'Someone take her photo when she's eating all these desserts so we can rib her about it later,' said Aunty V, with a grin.

For some reason, the thought of a photo sobered me up. It made me think of people who were no longer with us and although no one close to me had died, I was suddenly terrified of Ma dying.

'No,' I said. 'No photos.'

I didn't explain although everyone looked at me strangely.

15

For the next couple of days, we settled into a strange sort of routine. I didn't know if I liked it or hated it. With Aunty V, the house had been boisterous and fun but with Raghu, the house seemed fuller and louder. I would go to college with great reluctance because my thoughts were centred at home.

When I left for college the next morning, Ma and Raghu were watching a movie on Netflix. At 7.30 a.m. And Ma was eating some sort of pancake thingy that Raghu had made for her. He looked ridiculously pleased with himself.

'Want some?' he asked.

I looked at him—loose green shorts, a threadbare light pink vest that had seen better days, his sleep-tousled hair, and a light stubble on his face—and I shook my head.

'No, thanks,' I said tightly.

I glanced at Ma, who was digging into those Nutella covered pancakes like there was an impending apocalypse, and I thought about the apocalypse growing inside her.

Raghu was focusing on the movie. He laughed at a scene while I put on my shoes. I looked up at him surreptitiously as I tied the laces. His eyes got all crinkly when he grinned and it made me feel warm inside. I didn't want to think why. I straightened up and he looked at me again.

'So, how come you're eating all this in the morning? Didn't you have morning sickness?' I asked Ma, tearing my gaze away from Raghu.

'Disappeared after the first trimester!' Ma looked jubilant.

The human body is strange.

'See you guys later!' I called out.

At the door, I turned back to take a look at Ma. She looked content. Raghu was sitting cross-legged on the sofa and snagged a piece of pancake from Ma's plate. She yanked her plate away and he laughed.

I walked away, trying not to think too hard about the turmoil inside me.

Nisha wanted to know everything about Raghu during our lunch break. I sensed Anirudh was bored or jealous that Nisha was showing so much interest in Raghu. He had a look of irritation on his face that kept growing as we talked and it actually amused me.

'You'll meet him on Saturday, right? At the movie. See for yourself,' I stalled.

'You know, you could have told me he's coming too!' he interrupted suddenly.

'Why?' Nisha asked confused.

'I don't know if I want to be there while the two of you act foolishly around him, like he's Curtis Stone,' he muttered.

Nisha and I looked at each other and we both burst out laughing. Anirudh was definitely jealous.

'Curtis Stone? Please!' I laughed but I felt my face heat up a little.

Raghu was obviously nothing like the hot Australian chef but he was certainly hot, I thought. Shit. Raghu wasn't just cute. He was hot. How had this happened?

I glanced up to see Nisha pinch Anirudh's cheeks.

'SO cute. You're jealous!' she said.

'I'm not!' he said, crossing his arms defensively. 'Why would I be?'

'Don't worry. You'll always be my Sheldon Cooper,' she said, tweaking his ear. Anirudh narrowed his eyes, but by then Nisha had turned to me.

'Did Raghu ask you why you stopped talking to him?'

Nisha was like a terrier. Never letting go of the topic.

I sighed. 'Sort of. He tried to bring it up, but I didn't want to talk about it,' I said.

'But why? It would have been closure for you Ananya,' she said earnestly.

'Closure from what?' I asked her, shrugging. 'I'm no longer angry with him. So we can just put it behind us now.'

'Yes, but you didn't talk to him for years. Because he dated the girl who was horrible to you.'

I grimaced. It sounded ridiculous when she put it like that.

'Um, please. He was just part of that phase and I didn't want reminders,' I protested. 'We were kids.'

'We still are,' Anirudh said importantly.

'Oh yeah?' Nisha asked him, narrowing her eyes. 'Remind me the next time you want to . . . '

Want to what? Shit. I didn't want to hear this and Anirudh's face had turned a deep red but Nisha didn't elaborate.

I was still getting used to them being together and this conversation was making it all sorts of awkward. Thankfully, Nisha came back to me.

'So okay, the past is the past, but what about now? Does he have a girlfriend? Is he single?' Nisha was relentless.

I caught Anirudh's eyeroll and grinned. 'I don't know!' I said. 'I didn't ask. And I don't really care.'

I sipped water from my bottle, wondering if my lie was evident.

Nisha knew me too well. She gave me a knowing look and shook her head.

'Today's masala dosa is very good,' she said casually as she broke off a piece and ate it.

'Good,' I said, getting up from there. 'I have my lunch with me.'

I showed her my packet of crackers, the bland tasteless things that had been my college lunch for the longest time. She made a face and an exasperated sound. I never gave it a second thought normally, but today I was thinking about the lunch at home.

Aunty V loved to cook and going by what I'd seen of Raghu, he loved it too. He must have woken up at some unearthly hour to make pancakes for Ma. Together, the mother-son duo would have cooked like crazy today. I wondered just how hard it was going to get to resist their combined efforts when I went back home today. Despite that apprehension, I had a smile on my face and I realized it was there because of Raghu.

Suddenly, I was dreading this Saturday movie. Nisha was bound to notice things that no one else would. And later, she would make me talk about what I'd known since the moment I opened the door to Raghu yesterday afternoon.

I was crushing on him. Really badly.

16

'Why can't we go in Uncle's car?' Raghu asked, flipping through a magazine on my bed.

I looked at him from my dressing table mirror, as I combed my hair out and wondered if I should braid it or leave it untied. Raghu had just walked in, unannounced, and sprawled on my bed and I didn't want to make a big deal by telling him to leave. My discomfort at having him in my room, where he seemed to be taking up *all* the oxygen, should have been evident to him. He seemed unaffected though.

'You'll go crazy trying to find parking,' I remarked.

'But it's in a mall. Why wouldn't there be parking?' he asked, looking at my reflection in the mirror.

I looked away from his gaze. My acknowledgment of this crush had just made it all the more difficult to endure this movie outing now.

'Let's just take an auto and go. It's no big deal,' I said, wishing he'd get up and leave. I was feeling extremely self-conscious about even doing my usual make-up routine of kajal and lip gloss.

'Fine,' he said. 'Uncle's not going to let me drive his car anyway.'

I smiled. He was right. Papa was quite possessive about his car.

I observed him quietly in the mirror. He was wearing a black t-shirt that had a quote on it and jeans. He looked extremely comfortable on my bed, outstretched sideways with his long legs hanging off the edge.

There was nothing wrong in him sitting here like this, I told myself. It wasn't *his* fault that I was having inappropriate thoughts. I shushed them away and tried to focus on my face.

What did Raghu see when he saw me? Did he still see his fat friend from five years ago? My weight loss was not obvious and I was still uncomfortable about my body, and I was sure that my discomfort showed. How he saw me didn't matter at all, I told myself sternly, because nothing was going to come of this dumb crush.

I looked at my reflection in the mirror. Boys probably just saw hot or not and I obviously was not hot because he'd seen me at my worst. And I doubted he'd ever forget the sight of me stuck under the table. Ms Piggy. I was desperate for the day I would have visible cheekbones *and* collarbones. My shoulders were too round and my bust attracted the wrong sort of attention so I tried to downplay it. I knew that my legs were toned, but the rest of me was still Fat Ananya.

'We're getting late,' I told him shortly, my mood becoming glum. I capped my lipgloss and turned to face him.

'Hmm?'

'I said we're getting late. Get your ass off my bed so we can leave.'

'Eh. Okay, whatever,' he said, getting up and stretching.

I didn't want to notice him or his lean and long body so I turned and examined my face in the mirror again, hoping he wouldn't notice and tease me.

'Why is Bangalore so hot in February?' he asked as he pulled away his t-shirt from his back and straightened his shoulders, doing a little jig under the fan.

Aaaaaa. Because you're here, I yelled at him in my head.

I made a face and shrugged. 'I'll ask the weather gods and update you.'

He snorted and walked out of the room and I followed him. I checked my phone as we walked out. Nisha had messaged saying she was DYING to meet Raghu. Ugh.

The four of us didn't hit it off immediately. I was too concerned about what Nisha was going to say to me about him later and I froze with anxiety after introducing everyone. I watched Anirudh and Raghu chat with each other in that measured way that guys have.

Nisha frowned and turned to me. 'Why didn't you say he was cute?' she asked me in a whisper, raising one eyebrow.

'Because I don't think he is cute?' I said, making a face.

All around me, the smells of popcorn and nachos wafted in the air, tempting me endlessly. I pulled in my stomach without even realizing I was doing it.

'Liar. Just look at that cheeky grin,' she said in my ear.

I looked. He was indeed grinning in a very cocky way at something that Anirudh was saying. Anirudh being the equivalent of a sixty-year-old grandpa when it came to education was grilling Raghu about why he hadn't joined college after his twelfth and how could he be so chill about taking a year off. The fact that Raghu was so easy-going about his education was riling up Anirudh, who had been gunning to become a doctor from even before we had met. It wasn't just his dream. It was the collective dream of his entire family.

'It's all right, dude. My mom is freaked out, but one year this way or that isn't going to ruin my life,' Raghu said, smiling and shaking his head.

Anirudh glanced at me with a disbelieving look. I nodded at him, but I wasn't annoyed by Raghu's take-it-easy manner. I was irked at my own lack of ambition or rather my confusion.

Since the movie was about to begin, we strolled inside, taking the 3D glasses from the counter. Anirudh and Raghu started to bond when they discovered that they both supported Liverpool FC. I think Anirudh was finally able to stop thinking of Raghu as abnormal.

Since we had come to see a superhero movie, Nisha and Raghu got into an argument over different fandoms with Raghu telling Nisha that Marvel was overrated shit.

Nisha nearly choked on her popcorn. 'You don't really believe that!' she accused him.

'How do you know what I believe or not?' Raghu drawled, enjoying riling her up.

Anirudh frowned. He had noticed the high spots of colour on Nisha's face. He opened his mouth to intervene when she started talking rapidly, leaning forward and sideways in her seat to address Raghu.

'You just want to be seen as swimming against the tide. That's why you haven't joined any college. Not because you want to become a big chef,' she said.

Raghu frowned. I mentally facepalmed. Raghu hadn't told them about his dreams of becoming a chef. I had told Nisha about that. Why did she have to throw it in his face?

But before he could respond, the lights went out and the movie began. Raghu was sitting next to me and

I knew what Nisha said had affected him. He sat stiffly for the first half hour and I felt sick to my stomach. He was going to think I talked about him to my friends and, well, I did, but I didn't want him to know that!

Nisha, who was sitting on my other side, whispered in my ear. 'I'm so sorry. I shouldn't have said that.'

I didn't reply. I glanced at Raghu who was glaring at the screen.

By the time it was intermission, Raghu seemed fine. He got up to get some more popcorn and asked if I wanted some.

'No,' I told him.

He didn't look at Nisha as he walked past her to reach the aisle and walk downstairs.

'He's upset about what I said,' Nisha groaned. 'I should have kept my mouth shut.'

'He'll be fine,' I told her, although I wasn't sure.

I stood up because I wanted to go to the restroom. She joined me and we walked out together.

'What was I thinking? I don't even know him and I said all that to him.' She sounded rueful.

'It's okay,' I assured her. 'He needs to be taken down a peg or two anyway. Such an overconfident ass.'

'Who happens to have such a delectable ass,' Nisha said with a grin.

I felt my face flame up for the barest of seconds before I turned to her. 'Ugh,' I said, making a face and shuddering at the same time.

She frowned and I knew I had overdone it.

'So, this was the same guy whom you couldn't stand until a week ago,' she said, as I headed inside one of the stalls.

I shut my eyes, knowing that she had too much insight into my thoughts. When I stepped outside to wash my hands, she continued.

'So have you decided?' she asked, catching me off guard as I wiped my hands on a paper towel.

'Huh?'

'Whether you hate him or like him?'

I threw away the wadded paper towel and faced her.

'How does it matter?' I asked her finally.

'What do you mean?'

'Should I list the reasons why it doesn't matter?' I asked impatiently. It was fine for me to acknowledge this annoying crush I had on him, but I really didn't want to dissect it with Nisha. It would just make it worse if she agreed with me.

'Yes. Please do,' she said with a frown on her face.

We walked back to the auditorium where the movie was being screened while I enumerated the reasons in a whisper, counting off on my fingers.

'One, he doesn't see me as anything other than his fat friend who got stuck under a table at his ex-girlfriend's birthday party. Two, I was a fat blob then and I'm just a slightly less fat blob now. Three, I don't think he even sees me as a girl.'

Nisha stared at me solemnly for a few seconds and her eyes filled up with tears. I frowned. How had my words hurt *her*?

She shook her head. 'I wish you wouldn't hate yourself so much Ananya,' she whispered with a sniffle and turned away, walking into the dark auditorium.

I followed her, my heart thumping loudly. We never talked about how much I hated myself because it was uncomfortable, but sometimes, seeing her with Anirudh, the two of them so obviously happy with each other, made that knife twist a little deeper into my heart.

Who would look at you like that, I scoffed to myself. Raghu? I doubted that would ever happen, which was why it was pointless to think of whether I liked him or not.

I didn't pay attention to the rest of the movie because I was too aware of Raghu sitting beside me, and Nisha on my other side. It felt as though she was judging me.

My mind felt cluttered. Maybe that was why when Raghu offered me some of his popcorn, I put my hand inside the big tub without thinking and took out a handful and started eating.

The buttery, salty taste of the popcorn was shockingly good and it was only then that I realized that I was eating popcorn after years. The popcorn felt like it was blooming in my stomach, like it was a seed growing out, stretching, expanding.

It was all right. It was just some popcorn. I told myself that repeatedly to get over the anxiety that I had taught myself to feel whenever I ate anything that was even remotely tasty. The thoughts kept eroding whatever feelings of happiness I'd started the day with. I just wanted to go home.

When the movie ended, Nisha awkwardly addressed Raghu as we walked out. 'Hey, I'm sorry.'

'For what?' he asked.

'About earlier. I didn't mean to be rude,' she said with a shrug.

Anirudh threaded his fingers with hers and squeezed. I don't know if Raghu noticed it, but I did.

'It's all right,' Raghu replied, looking away. I knew him well enough to know that it wasn't true.

This movie expedition had been a disaster. We got into an auto outside the mall and left. On the way back, I felt like I had to explain Nisha's actions or at least try to do it.

'About your chef thing . . . I . . . I end up telling Nisha everything,' I told him, hoping he would understand. 'I didn't realize that . . .'

'Maybe I should ask her then,' he interrupted, his eyes blazing, 'why you stopped talking to me five years ago.'

I felt my stomach fall away. I opened my mouth but couldn't bring myself to actually say anything.

'Why does it matter so much?' I asked him finally. I couldn't imagine having to tell him why I had distanced myself from him and revisit my humiliation, or make him realize how he was connected with all of it in my mind.

'You were my friend, Ananya. One of my only friends,' he said flatly.

'You had Esha, no?' I snapped, unable to stop myself.

He froze and looked at me briefly before turning away. We didn't speak for the rest of the ride home.

17

At dinner that night, Raghu announced that he wanted to go back to Mumbai the next day. My heart sank. I had hoped that he would stay a while longer. Even Aunty V was surprised.

'But I was speaking to people for a restaurant apprenticeship for you,' she protested.

He shrugged. 'I'll come back when there's something happening for certain.'

Stay, I wanted to tell him. I was having fun with him in the house and even though things had been awkward after the movie, I still wanted him around.

'Arrey, it's almost certain. I've spoken to a friend of mine who knows a lot of people and I'm meeting her soon. She'll get you an apprenticeship somewhere for sure,' Aunty V said.

'Fine. So I'll come be back then. Better still, ask her to find something for me in Mumbai,' he said.

Aunty V frowned. 'That's not how it works,' she said firmly.

Before he could protest, she spoke again, 'We're doing our college reunion here, in the house and we need all the help we can get.'

He looked at me then and I made a face but also smiled. The reunion sounded terrible but I would be able to tolerate it if he was around. He hadn't spoken a word to me after my outburst in the auto. He didn't return the smile and looked away.

'That's two weekends away,' he said finally. 'You want me to stay here till then?'

'Yes,' Aunty V said flatly. 'There's a lot of work that needs to be done.'

I glanced at Ma, who looked like she was happy that she had relinquished everything to Aunty V.

'Why are you doing all this, Mom? Don't you know that Ananya has her finals next month? And Aunty Chitra doesn't need all this excitement and stress,' Raghu said.

I was startled at hearing my name in the middle of their argument.

Aunty V looked conflicted, but I found myself speaking. 'No, it's okay. If this is what Ma wants, then we'll do it.'

Papa looked at me contemplatively, probably wondering how I was being so calm. He didn't have to know about my ulterior motives and I actually didn't know what they were either.

'Fine, then find me the apprenticeship soon. I don't want to be sitting around at home all day,' Raghu said, getting up from the dining table with his plate.

'I don't know if this generation is lazy or entitled, Chitra,' Aunty V was saying as I got up too and followed him to the kitchen.

Maybe Raghu and I did need to talk after all. Maybe talking about the past would ease the hurt and pain and we could be friends again. And he needn't ever know about my crush.

'Can we talk?' I asked him.

He looked at me as he washed his plate, eyebrows raised. '*Now* you want to talk?'

I nodded. It was hot and stuffy inside the house.

'Let's go to the garden,' I suggested and opened the kitchen back door that led outside. Wordlessly, he followed me.

The starless night surrounded us and I could smell raat ki rani blossoms. Papa had kept a bench in the garden, where he planned to read the newspaper on weekend mornings. He never did, but sometimes, I came out here to read.

I didn't know how to begin. This was awkward, but I really wanted to put it past us and move ahead.

I took a deep breath. 'So, Esha's birthday five years ago . . .' I said and looked at him sideways. He looked at me steadily, but I could sense him tensing.

'You remember what happened, right?' I asked, looking down at my knuckles.

'Yeah, I do,' he said softly.

I winced the slightest bit. 'I was mortified, Raghu. I wanted to die. I was that embarrassed.' I spoke softly.

He exhaled loudly. 'Yes, but . . . I was your friend. I came to ask you why you ran away from there and wanted both of us to confront Esha and ask her how she could talk like that. But you didn't even open the door,' he said.

What? I looked at him in surprise.

'Don't lie,' I snapped.

He flinched as though I'd slapped him. 'Why would I lie?' he asked.

'Because . . . because she . . . wasn't she your girlfriend later on?' I asked, my nostrils flaring.

'How did you know about that?' he asked, looking embarrassed.

'I heard her talking about it with a friend. So if she was your girlfriend,' I continued angrily but he put his hand over mine and I stopped talking briefly, as his touch ignited something on the surface of my skin. I was scared too figure out what that was and I pulled out my hand from under his.

'Wait,' he said.

I shook my head. 'You were my friend too, Raghu,' I said, my voice thick with unshed tears. I cleared my throat unsuccessfully and found that my eyes had filled up with tears, much to my horror. I wiped them away quickly and took a deep breath. This had to be said.

'But then you asked her to be your girlfriend . . .' I was having so much trouble speaking.

He was shaking his head rapidly.

'No . . . it seems so stupid now. But . . .' he breathed out, rubbing his forehead with his palm.

'What?' I asked.

'I was such an idiot back then,' he said in a low voice.

'What do you mean?'

'I was planning to take revenge on her for being mean to you,' he said quickly, closing his eyes.

I stared back at him, not believing his words but the expression on his face — embarrassment mixed with shame — had me covering my own mouth with my hand, trying to quell the disbelieving laughter that was threatening to bubble through.

He opened one eye and then the other. 'I was such an idiot,' he repeated in a whisper.

That he had been thinking of me, even during his silly plan of revenge was making me happy. I punched his arm.

'You still are,' I said.

'So you stopped talking to me because of that?' He looked like a great weight had been lifted from his shoulders and I felt the same too.

Before I could answer, he got up. 'Let's go for a walk!'

'Now?' I asked, surprised.

He nodded and walked towards the back gate. I called out to Ma and told her before following him. We walked in silence for a bit. The moonlit night and the trees lining the road made it all very romantic.

I was feeling a burst of happiness so intense that I could never remember feeling something like it, and I didn't want it to stop. But his question hung between us.

'Yeah, well, I just couldn't face you,' I said.

He bumped his shoulder with mine. I stifled my annoyance at him for being completely unaware of how everything he did played havoc with my head and my senses.

'That's silly. I wish we'd spoken about it before and cleared the air. But I'm glad we got the chance now.' He smiled at me and I felt it like a sucker punch to my stomach. My mouth went dry.

'Let's go back home,' I told him, turning back.

'What? Already? Let's walk around a bit more,' he insisted.

Shrugging, I tried to match my pace to his longer strides.

'What exactly did you mean by revenge?' I asked him. The word had been bugging me since he said it.

He scratched the side of his head and wrinkled his nose. 'Do we have to talk about that?'

I was suddenly wary. We had been kids back then, but what had Raghu done? Had he hurt her somehow? Despite my anger at her, I didn't want that. I didn't want Raghu to be that kind of a person.

'I'd like to know, yes,' I told him finally.

He looked sheepish. 'Silly things, man. Things to embarrass her more often than not,' he said with a slight shrug.

'Like what?' I persisted.

'Like I'd ask her to meet me for a movie, but I wouldn't show up. Or if I did, I'd be dressed very badly. I was quite mean to her when we went on a group outing with her friends,' he said, looking miserable.

'How mean?' I was glad that his 'revenge' had been petty and not cruel. But then . . . words are cruel too. This deflated my happiness a little. I realized that I wanted revenge when I was the one meting it out. I didn't want Raghu to step in and defend me.

'I said nasty things about how she dressed,' he said, looking down. He was clearly ashamed of himself and I was disappointed too.

'And then?'

'She broke up with me,' he shrugged. 'Not that it mattered because I'd lost your friendship by then.'

He turned to me and we looked at each other. There was something different about this moment because he kept staring at me and I couldn't bring myself to look away. I felt warm and prickly at the same time, and a little breathless as well.

'I'm glad we're back to being friends now,' he said finally.

The spell broke and I nodded, not sure of what had just happened. I realized we were back at the house and I didn't wait for him as I walked inside. He followed me in silence.

I turned around, just before we went inside.

'I'm glad you're here,' I told him.

His brown eyes darkened and I stepped back in surprise, but he nodded.

When we went inside the house, I was nearly breathless with the need to talk to Nisha about what had happened. Raghu and I were back to being friends, but there was something else going on too. *I* had a crush on him, yes, but why was he looking at me strangely? I couldn't believe he was interested in me, so it must be something else, I thought.

All thoughts fled when we walked back inside the living room and Ma looked at me, her face pink and shining.

'Ananya! Where were you? I kept calling your number!'

I looked at her in panic. I hadn't taken my phone and gone out. Had something happened? Was it the baby? But Ma was just around five months pregnant. She couldn't be having it already. She didn't look very panicked though. In fact, Papa was beaming and Aunty V, too, was grinning away.

'What is it?' I asked, breathless.

Raghu followed me but right now, I wasn't thinking about him. I was worried for Ma and this stupid baby too.

'Come here?' she said and patted the sofa beside her. I sat down reluctantly.

'Do we need to go to the hospital?' I whispered. Were adults prone to grinning like maniacs at this time?

'Hospital? No no,' Papa assured me.

'Then?'

'Here,' Ma said, taking my hand and placing it lightly on the top of her rounded belly.

My eyes went wide when I realized what was happening. The part of me that went 'ewww' wanted to take my hand off immediately but then there was a light flutter, like a butterfly spreading its wings and taking flight. My mouth dropped open and Ma grinned at me.

'Is that . . .'

There was movement inside once more, a sort of squirming that made me realize the immensity of what Ma was dealing with. She nodded; her eyes shiny with tears.

'Is this the first time you're feeling it?' I asked in a whisper. I wished I was alone with Ma to share this special moment. That was silly. She was happy and she wanted to share it with her loved ones.

'Isn't it thrilling?' Aunty V interjected, even as Ma nodded.

I looked away and found Raghu looking at me, a smile on his face. I smiled back at him. Papa's look of embarrassment was tempered with pride. I couldn't stop grinning either.

'Can I feel it too?' Raghu asked.

Ma nodded and he came forward, kneeling on the ground before her and placed his palm on her stomach. He looked disappointed.

'Nothing,' he said.

'Arrey, you impatient fellow, wait,' Aunty V chided him.

He pouted, and then his eyes lit up. 'Oh my god! I felt it!' he gasped as he took his hand away from Ma's stomach.

His elation was contagious. We all laughed.

Just then, the gates creaked open and my eyes widened.

'Who's coming home at this time?' I asked as the doorbell rang.

'Oh! That must be the Swiggy guy,' Ma said happily.

'Huh?'

'I ordered Death by Chocolate from Corner House to celebrate,' she said.

I wasn't angry or annoyed at the mention of ice cream because at this moment, I was just ridiculously pleased with life.

'I hope you ordered enough for everyone,' I told Ma and she looked at me, surprised. I hadn't eaten ice cream in years.

'I did. You want some?' she asked.

I nodded. This moment called for a celebration. I would atone later.

18

Sunday went by in planning the reunion. But I didn't care. I was walking around the house, thrilled at the thought that Raghu was going to be here for the next two weeks. I had Death by Chocolate last night after years and it was as awesome as it had always been. I managed to stop after a couple of spoons.

I woke up and exercised for an extra half hour to compensate for it but I was feeling light inside. The self-hate, my companion for the past five years, didn't feel as heavy as it did before. Or maybe it was there but I had succeeded in pushing it into a corner for the moment.

Maybe it showed on my face because Raghu looked at me strangely. 'What's going on?' he asked me as he made breakfast for everyone. He was chopping onions quickly and efficiently and I admired how he did it—ruthless speed and excellent coordination.

Papa was sitting at the kitchen table and looked grumpy as he read the newspaper. I ignored him.

'Nothing,' I shrugged, as I got out the dosa maavu that Meena Akka had prepared and kept in the fridge and took it over to him. He had announced that he was making masala dosa and I had offered to help, just to spend a little extra time with him.

After lunch today, he was going to meet Aunty V's friend who had got him an interview with a chef at a restaurant in Indiranagar.

'You look happy.'

'I am,' I said, glancing over at Papa and then looking back at him. 'Anything you want me to do to help?'

'Peel the potatoes?'

Ma and Aunty V walked inside, still talking and joined Papa at the table. The two of us worked in companionable silence as our parents made plans for the reunion. Raghu shared a droll look with me and I grinned back at him.

Breakfast was amazing even though I ate only half a masala dosa.

'Let Ananya make some so you can eat too, Raghu,' Ma suggested.

I looked at her face, shiny with happiness. Her worry lines seemed to have faded and even though she was tired, she looked happy. I glanced at her stomach, at the life growing inside, and for the first time since this news, I felt protective, not just towards Ma but also towards that little thing inside, whatever it was—boy or girl. I no longer thought of it as 'that stupid baby'.

'Yeah, I'll make some for you,' I offered.

He shook his head. 'You haven't eaten yet.'

'Oh, I'm done,' I told him quickly. My stomach protested.

The masala he'd made for the potatoes was soft and not too spicy and he'd grated coconut over it. I could eat it from a bowl, like halwa, I thought, agonizing at the thought of actually doing that. I was a little dismayed at how often my thoughts were turning to food, now that both he and Aunty V were in the house.

'No problem. I'll join you guys in a bit,' he said.

I was bursting with the need to tell everything to Nisha, but I'd have to wait until we met tomorrow in college. I wanted to tell her in person to see her expression when I told her about that 'moment' with Raghu. I didn't want to think too much about it or read too much into it until I spoke to her.

After breakfast, Ma and Aunty V sat in the living room, and got on Facebook to invite their friends for the party. I helped out by making a poster for the invite. Then we started sending them out and, seriously, old people had nothing better to do on Sunday morning than being on Facebook because they all responded immediately. They were definitely going to come!

Raghu had gone to take a shower after breakfast. He emerged from his room, hair still wet and shiny.

Aunty V looked up and frowned. 'You need to dry your hair.'

'Ma, I'm not a kid!' he protested, looking a little embarrassed.

'Yes, you are,' she shot back at him.

'I won't catch a cold because of wet hair!' he said, his face a little red.

Since Aunty V kept glaring at him, he scowled and walked back to the bedroom. He came out with a towel tied on his head, turban style. He looked ridiculous and he knew it.

Aunty V took one look at him and slapped her forehead.

'This boy,' she mumbled as he sat down beside them.

Yes, this boy, I thought. I was glad he had come. Even if I was just his friend, I was glad of his company, of the fun he brought into our lives.

Papa hmphed and I turned to him.

'You've been weird all morning,' I said.

He looked at me and frowned. 'Stupid party,' he mumbled.

'Aww. Are you jealous that this Ashwin guy . . . no, *Ash* from Mom's college will be coming to the party?' Ash had been the first one to RSVP.

His face reddened. He cleared his throat. 'Nonsense. I'm just worried about your mother. I don't want her to get stressed over this party.'

'She won't,' I assured him. 'Look at her. She seems so much happier with something to look forward to.'

Ma indeed seemed to be better. I wouldn't say her face was glowing—she still had those zits and now dark circles too—but she seemed a lot happier.

'Thanks, Ananya,' Papa said suddenly.

'For what?'

'For everything. For the support. For being happy for us.'

I looked away because, along with guilt, there was something else. What did Papa mean by 'us'? That he and Ma and this baby were a family and I wasn't? No, I told myself immediately. That was a stupid thing to assume. Then I felt guilty again because I hadn't been supportive or happy at first.

'It's nothing,' I mumbled and looked away.

Raghu looked up from the laptop and raised his eyebrows in a silent question. I nodded, knowing I could talk to him about this. I mouthed 'later' at him.

I knew he was happier too, since we'd talked. I didn't know my friendship had mattered so much to him and it felt good. Very good, actually.

'What are we having for lunch?' Ma asked.

'We *just* had breakfast Ma,' I said.

'Yeah, but we're hungry.'

'Who's we?' I asked, puzzled.

'Baby and I,' she responded firmly.

'At your service, Aunty. What do you want?' Raghu asked, getting up.

'No, no! You just made breakfast for everyone,' Ma protested, looking guilty.

'It's okay. Let him get used to working his ass off,' Aunty V said, winking at me.

19

The next morning, I woke up at my usual time. I had to do yoga and get ready for college.

There was a knock on my door. I got out of bed and opened it. Raghu was standing outside, wearing trackpants and a t-shirt.

'Dude, come jogging with me,' he said.

I frowned. I wasn't comfortable exercising outside. 'Uh . . .'

'I know you have college but it's still early. You Bangalore guys are so lucky with these parks you have. I can't believe you want to sit cooped up in the house all the time,' he said, wrinkling his nose.

'I do not sit cooped up,' I protested. 'Fine. I'll join you in five minutes.'

To my surprise, the whole family was out, waiting for me. Huh?

'Fresh air is good for the baby and your Ma,' Aunty V said as she tied her shoelaces.

Papa, who never did any sort of exercise, looked grumpy. Ma smiled as she sat down on the low storage bench that housed all our shoes. She was breathing heavily, though we hadn't even begun walking.

Papa did something very sweet. He knelt down and helped Ma wear her shoes before she asked for assistance. She couldn't bend over these days with her stomach protruding so much.

Raghu, who was at the door looking impatient, looked at me—and there it was. That strange, charged moment again. I couldn't look away. He smiled at Ma who was coming up behind me, panting heavily.

'I'm going to slow you all down,' she said, shaking her head as we left the house and Papa locked up behind us.

'No one's in a race, Chitra,' Aunty V admonished her.

It was a lovely bright morning and the morning sun was just perfect for a walk in the park. There was one just around the corner from our house, but I'd never bothered going there. It seemed like a multitude of aunties and uncles were walking briskly or slowly in circles around the park's walkway.

'Come on!' Raghu urged me as he broke into a jog. Reluctantly, I joined him and we left our parents walking slowly on the path as we jogged together. Raghu was taller and I had to struggle to keep up with him. By the time we had done five rounds, my calves were protesting and my lungs were screaming. I was sweating buckets.

I saw that Ma and Aunty V were sitting on one of the benches and Papa wasn't with them. I slowed down near them and Raghu frowned.

'You're done already?' he asked as he slowed down too. He was sweating too but apart from that, he seemed perfectly fine. I could barely talk as I collapsed on the bench with Aunty V and Ma.

'You go on,' I said wheezing.

'Here,' Ma offered me a bottle of water and I gulped it down gratefully.

'Easy,' Aunty V said, patting my back.

I was going to kill Raghu, I thought, as I saw him jog away. I liked to exercise at home, and I had thought I was fit with my yoga and my exercise apps that I used to work out every day. But I'd thought wrong. Slowly, my breathing came back to normal.

'Where's Papa?' I asked.

Ma indicated another bench where he was surrounded by other uncles. Papa was relating something and they were all laughing.

I checked my phone and saw that I barely had time to get back home to get ready and leave for college.

'Ma, give me the keys. I need to get changed for college,' I said, getting up from there.

'We'll all come,' she said, getting up.

'No, stay here. Enjoy the sun and the air,' I told her with a smile.

I took the keys from her and quickly left the park. Raghu hadn't seen me leave and I hastened back where I took a shower and got ready. I felt flushed with energy. But more than anything else, I was feeling very hungry.

My battle with food had resulted in me learning to control my hunger pangs, learning to push them down, ignore them or satisfy them with fruit or crackers. But now, I found my feet moving to the kitchen. I opened the fridge and found the leftover potato masala from yesterday. I found the dosa maavu too and before I could stop to think, I was making a masala dosa for myself.

I sat down in the empty kitchen and looked at the plate, my mouth watering. I broke off the crispy edge and ate a bite, and then pushed away the plate, feeling sick suddenly.

I was heading down that path again. The path that had made me Fat Ananya and Ms Piggy. With Raghu making everything look so easy in the kitchen, I'd forgotten how much I loved baking. I couldn't go back there. I was still just halfway to my goal and I couldn't keep falling back, I scolded myself.

I folded the masala dosa into a foil wrapper and decided to give it to Nisha or Anirudh. I left for college before Ma and the others returned.

Raghu's interview with a somewhat famous chef had gone well and he was going to start his internship there today.

I would probably see less of him now, I thought with disappointment. I also needed to figure out all these weird feelings I had around him and I needed to talk to Nisha about it.

Once I was in college, I could barely wait for a free period for us to talk. But when it was time, I couldn't bring myself to say the words.

What would I tell her? That I had a crush on Raghu? That we'd been having these weird moments where he'd stare intensely at me and wouldn't look away? Moments that left me feeling as if the breath had been knocked out from my body completely?

'What is it?' she asked finally. We were in an empty classroom and I'd told them I wanted to talk so we had strolled inside and sat down on the benches.

'Raghu and I talked,' I said finally. Her eyebrows went up and she looked at Anirudh.

'And?' she asked me, looking expectant.

Feeling somewhat foolish, I told them about how Raghu and I had put our differences aside. That we'd talked about everything and his 'revenge' plan.

Nisha was looking at me avidly as I narrated everything. To my surprise, Anirudh leaned forward, cocking his head slightly.

'You like him,' he said.

'Huh?' I asked, feeling a blush creep onto my cheeks.

He nodded and smiled. 'You *definitely* like him,' he said.

I turned to Nisha for help, but she smiled in an irritatingly wise manner.

'So what?' I shrugged. 'I'm sure there are hundreds of girls who like him too.'

'True . . . but . . .' Nisha looked somewhat stricken. Maybe she was remembering the things I'd told her about why my crush on him was pointless. I was certainly remembering my words

Suddenly, I didn't want to tell them about those moments I'd shared with him. Maybe I was reading too much into it. Maybe he'd just spaced out and I happened to be in his line of sight.

I changed the topic swiftly to the reunion being planned at home. 'Can you believe they're thrilled about it? Imagine meeting everyone after more than twenty years.'

'I think that would be nice,' Anirudh said, with a faraway look in his eyes, as though he was picturing it.

'It would be if you've achieved something in life. What if you haven't done anything worthwhile?'

'Um, your mom has achieved a lot okay? She's heading corporate communications at a big software firm. So I don't know where you're going with this,' Nisha frowned.

'No, not Ma,' I said hastily.

'Even Aunty V sounds super cool,' Nisha stated.

I made a face and exhaled loudly. 'No, it's not them. I was just thinking about us,' I said finally.

'What about us?' she asked.

'If we were to meet after twenty years, you . . . you're going to be a great architect and Anirudh will be a successful doctor and, who knows, maybe the two of you will be married and have a bunch of cute and geeky kids. While I will have no idea what I would be,' I said softly. I didn't add that I might probably be alone and still fat.

Anirudh's mouth dropped open. Then, with a funny look on his face, he turned to Nisha. 'How many is a bunch?' he choked out.

Nisha rolled her eyes and laughed. '*That's* your takeaway from what Ananya said?' she asked him, shoving at him.

He scratched the side of his head and smiled at me. 'You're so mad, Ananya. Worrying about something that is twenty years away! And now you've got me thinking about *all* the possibilities,' he said.

Nisha rolled her eyes and turned to me again. 'It's all right if you don't have it all figured out.'

'Easy for you to say,' I remarked. 'But . . . what if I don't find what I want to do? What if I just waste my time and never accomplish anything?'

Nisha shook her head. 'Give it time. You don't have to be clued in right away. It will come to you.'

I didn't reply to that because the bell rang and a group of boys and girls came inside for the next class. As we got up and left, I realized I was still resentful of how the two of them, and even Raghu, knew what they wanted to do with their lives.

20

The next two weeks went by in a flurry of activity. I thought I wouldn't see much of Raghu but he kept surprising me by insisting that we go to the park every morning. Some days we walked briskly, some days we jogged, and some days we sat down on a park bench and played chess. Ma, Papa and Aunty V joined us sometimes.

Though I didn't get to see him during the day, every night I went to sleep thinking about the following morning when we would meet again. It was almost magical. I left for college every morning in a great mood. At the same time, it was as if I was waiting for the other shoe to drop.

We didn't have any more of *those* moments again and I was disappointed because it confirmed my theory about it being a figment of my imagination. We laughed a lot and sometimes, when it was just the two of us, sitting on the park bench and talking, I'd feel all those years and that anger melt away, making me wish I hadn't wasted all that time *not* talking to him.

We exchanged phone numbers and whenever he was free during the day, he would send me funny memes and I would hunt around for one to send back to him. This had become our thing now. I'd seen Nisha give me a knowing look whenever she spotted me texting him, but thankfully, she didn't say anything. I wasn't ready yet to label our relationship.

The reunion party was happening that night and Raghu had taken the day off. I was also home since it was Saturday and Ma had been after me to clean the house properly along with Meena Akka.

Everyone was in an irritable mood. Papa was harrumphing around the house, muttering to himself about Aunty V's hare-brained ideas and Aunty V was snapping back at him whenever she heard him mutter her name.

When I was done cleaning the house, Ma informed me that the party was going to happen in the garden outside because of the 'sultry weather'. Her words, not mine.

'What? Why did you make me clean the house then?' I asked, pushing the sweaty strands of hair from my face. My t-shirt had wet blotches on the back.

'Because people will come inside the house too!' Ma replied. 'I mean, they'll come inside to use the restroom or . . . you never know.'

Shaking my head, I rushed to my room to quickly shower. I changed into another t-shirt and I tugged on a pair of shorts. Then I stopped. I wore shorts when I exercised in my room and sometimes, very rarely, when I sat outside with Ma and Papa, who didn't think anything of it. I was suddenly self-conscious of wearing shorts with Raghu and Aunty V around.

I stared at my body in the mirror. I was not Fat Ananya from before. But I wasn't Skinny Ananya either. I squeezed my eyes shut and opened them again. I didn't look weird, so Raghu wouldn't laugh at me. I doubt he'd even notice me, since he'd be busy cooking. I took a deep breath and walked to the kitchen.

In the kitchen, Raghu was facing the counter and he was wearing a bandana over his head. He had a wireless headset on and he was dancing weirdly.

I tapped his shoulder lightly. He whirled around in surprise and gave me such a huge smile that my heart lurched painfully. He took off the headset and switched it off, blinking at me.

'Finally, you've come to help. Took you long enough,' he said mock sternly.

'Ma had me clean the whole house and *then* she tells me that the party is outside! I'm so sorry!' I said, batting my eyelashes in an over-the-top manner, hoping to make him laugh.

He frowned instead and cleared his throat. 'Fine. Um.'

'You all right?' I asked him.

'Yeah. Yeah, of course. Are you wearing perfume?' he asked suddenly.

I shrugged. 'I always do.'

He nodded briskly and then directed me to prepare the shortcrust bases for the savoury tarts he was making as appetizer. Ma had refused to let him cook for everyone and she had ordered food from outside, but Raghu had insisted on making the appetisers and dessert.

We worked in silence and Aunty V came in to check on us a few times. The chocolate ganache tart was her speciality, but Raghu was making it this time.

Over the past few days, with Raghu at home, I found myself spending time more and more in the kitchen, irresistibly drawn to cooking and baking again, but barely tasting anything. I don't know if Raghu had noticed it but I was making a huge concession for him and I really didn't want him to make a big deal about me not eating anything he cooked.

I might have to give in today, I thought, as I rolled out the tarts and lined them in the tart cases. The ganache he was stirring smelled heavenly.

I found Raghu looking at me every now and then. I was suddenly worried that maybe he *did* find it strange that I was in shorts. My heart sank, but I decided to ask him about it. We were friends, right?

I put my hands on my hips.

'What's wrong?' I asked him. 'Have I got flour on my head?'

He looked a little stricken as he shook his head. 'No. It's nothing.'

Shrugging, I went back to my work. It was hot and I was sweating again and would need another shower after this, but it didn't matter as long as I got to spend more time with him.

I looked up at him to find him looking at me once more. He smiled at me.

21

When Ma's friends from college started showing up, there was much excited chatter and shrieking.

Papa was sitting in the garden, checking something on his phone while Ma and Aunty V were catching up with their old classmates. I could see some of the action from the kitchen window that looked out to a part of the garden.

Raghu and I finally finished working in the kitchen. Ma wanted me to come and meet her friends, but I had to take another shower and get dressed before that.

'You're also coming to meet them, right?' I asked him, as I dusted my palms and put away things we'd used.

'No way,' he replied. 'I'm going to crash. I haven't slept this early since I started helping at the restaurant.'

My stomach plummeted in disappointment. 'But what about dinner?' I asked.

'Not hungry. I'll come and grab something from the kitchen later,' he said, waving at me as he headed off to the guest room.

I stood there for a few seconds, as he disappeared from view. I rubbed my face. I was being stupid. I had a life of my own. Raghu would go back to Mumbai. I had to get used to him not being around, I thought. But at the same time, I didn't want to spend time with these aunties and uncles who were chattering away outside with Ma and Aunty V if Raghu wasn't there.

I had to at least say hi to them, I thought despondently. Ma wouldn't like it if I decided not to show up.

I went to my room, took a quick shower, and searched my wardrobe for something to wear. My eyes fell on the green dress I had got for my birthday. It wasn't too dressy but it was sort of formal-ish and Ma had liked it when I had worn it.

I slipped the dress over my head and I winced when I realized it was tighter than it had been that day. My eyes filled up with tears and I sat on the bed and took a deep breath.

I forced myself to look in the mirror. This was what Raghu saw when he saw me. My fat arms, my thick ankles, my sturdy calves. But he wasn't going to be there, was he? He said he was going to sleep. I sucked my stomach in and wiped the tears from my face.

Then, almost mechanically, I put on some make up, because I'd found that if I made the effort to look pretty, people tended not to notice my body. I brushed my hair out over my shoulders. I debated whether to wear a stole and decided not to. I had looked ridiculous on my birthday and I would look even more so now, because it was so hot outside.

I tried to ignore the nervousness and anxiety that roiled inside me. Fat Ananya, the voice whispered and I shushed it.

I needed Fat Ananya to leave. To be gone for good. But as I glanced one last time at the mirror before stepping outside, I knew she was still there.

Unnerved, I pushed open my door and walked outside. I could hear the sounds of laughter from outside the house and I walked there, my gaze lingering on the corridor where the guest room was, where Raghu was probably snoring away obliviously.

Aunty V had got fairy lights strung around the garden, and we'd hired some tables and chairs that were scattered around. I looked around at the people who had come. Some looked much older than my mother and some looked quite young.

Ma was sitting at one of the tables, talking to someone I recognized from the photos on Facebook. It was that man Ashwin—or Ash—who was talking to her in a low voice and going by the look on Ma's face, she seemed to be enjoying herself.

Amused, I looked around. Aunty V was surrounded by a group of people and she was relating something funny to them.

Papa walked towards me, his face grumpy.

'What is it?' I asked him.

'Nothing. I'm bored,' he said, glancing at the table where Ma and Ashwin were talking.

'You're jealous,' I stated.

He rolled his eyes. 'I'm not jealous. I'm really bored. I don't know these people at all,' he said. 'I think I'll go inside and watch TV.'

'But that's rude,' I protested.

He sighed. 'So what should I do? Sit here in a corner? I've already had quite a bit to drink.'

'Sit in the corner and I'll join you as soon as I go and meet everyone,' I told him.

He walked back and sat down on the chair and suddenly his face brightened. I turned to look at what had caused the change of expression. It was Raghu, standing at the door, hands in his pockets. My heart fluttered in my chest.

He'd changed into loose-fitting cargo shorts and paired it with a white T-shirt. He surveyed the scene and then saw Papa, who was waving at him. Smiling, he walked towards him.

I didn't think he had seen me so I walked towards Ma to say hello to Ashwin and other people she wanted me to meet.

Ashwin was soft-spoken and shy and not at all the hot dude Ma and Aunty V had made him out to be. Ma was glowing, though, as she spoke to him. She was wearing a light yellow kurta and loose pink palazzo pants. She had left her hair loose and I was startled to realize she was looking pretty. She'd managed to hide the dark circles and zits with concealer and her voice had a special sort of quality as she laughed. She never laughed like this with us, I thought, this tinkling, breathless sort of laugh.

I joined Papa and Raghu. Raghu, who was checking his phone, looked at me in surprise.

'I thought you were going to sleep!' I announced as I sat down.

Raghu blinked a couple of times. 'I was. Then Mom called me and asked me to come out for a bit.' He looked down again at his phone.

I looked at the curve of his neck, at his hair still damp from a shower and felt the strangest longing to run my hand through his hair.

Great idea, having these thoughts with Papa sitting at the same table!

'And you came and sat here instead of meeting your mother's friends?' I asked him, willing him to look up.

He grunted. 'I'll meet them in a bit,' he muttered.

I heard a snore. Papa had fallen asleep, and his head was on the table.

Raghu looked up and his eyes met mine. I thought he was going to grin but he kept looking at me with a serious expression. My stomach contracted and my mouth went dry. He looked away, and I could breathe once more.

'Papa's had too much to drink,' I remarked, trying to keep the conversation neutral with him.

He didn't say anything, but he put his phone away.

'Should we try and take him inside?' I asked.

He looked at me again, but this time it was an expression I was used to. 'You serious? We could dislocate something carrying him inside,' he said, grinning.

'I know. And it would embarrass Ma too,' I said, shaking my head.

He sighed. 'I think I'll go and say hi to these people and then head back inside to sleep,' he said, still not making a move to get up.

'It's kind of weird seeing Ma and Aunty V behave like young girls,' I said.

'I know. Look at my mom. She's the life of the party,' he remarked.

'Really! And my mom, I haven't seen her look this pretty ever before,' I said as I looked at her and smiled. She was now talking to some other people but there was a shine in her eyes and it was heart-warming to see her like this.

'Yeah. Very pretty,' Raghu said.

I looked at him. He was looking at me, not at Ma.

22

Raghu didn't go to sleep. Instead, we hung around. We tried to wake Papa up when Aunty V served dinner, but he kept snoring.

I was feeling anxious because Raghu and I kept having these moments, where Raghu would look at me with a strange expression, which made me think . . .

I looked at my phone and wondered if I could quickly relay everything to Nisha. What was happening here? I needed some female perspective. Why was he looking at me every now and then? Did he think I was pretty? Because I was in a dress and I was wearing make-up? But we'd been having these moments from the night he and I talked about Esha.

I barely ate anything. This wasn't the time to call Nisha. That would have to wait.

I overheard a couple of women sniggering at something and I frowned. Raghu's expression changed too when he overheard what they were saying. They were talking about my mother's pregnancy, and laughing at her.

Raghu's face darkened as phrases like 'at her age', 'fat' and 'what was she thinking' floated towards us. What was wrong with people, I thought, incensed. Ma was not too old to have a baby!

'I can't believe these women have the gall to come to Aunty Chitra's party and make fun of her!' Raghu snapped.

I nodded angrily. How dare they!

'I have half a mind to go and tell them that at least Aunty Chitra has a reason to put on weight. What's their excuse?' he said, pushing away his chair slightly and rising.

What? No. That wasn't right. He did not just say that.

'Wait!' I said immediately, putting out my hand and holding his wrist.

He looked down at my hand and I pulled it away, feeling silly. But this needed to be said.

'Don't do that, Raghu. You can't fat-shame someone,' I said.

He looked confused and then understanding dawned, along with shame.

'I'm sorry,' he said sitting down, his gaze lowered.

I looked at his bent head and smiled in relief.

'I've never forgotten the words Esha said about me,' I told him quietly.

He looked up at me then, his face troubled. We hadn't talked about this the other night. We had glossed over it and I had hoped I would never have to bring it up. But I wanted him to understand that Esha's body shaming had become a part of me.

'I've lived with those words these past few years, reminding myself of them whenever I felt myself craving food,' I said. 'Fat bitch. Ugly cow. Ms Piggy.'

His eyes grew wide and he shook his head.

I didn't let him speak. 'I've worked so hard all these years to stop hearing those words whenever I see myself in the mirror, Raghu, but I still hear them sometimes.'

'You're none of those things,' he said in a fierce whisper as he leaned forward and covered my hand with his.

My heart leapt.

Papa let out a big snore and we were both startled. We had almost forgotten that Papa was still at the table.

I felt idiotic, bringing all that up *now*. I desperately wanted to change the subject. I looked at Raghu, pleading with my eyes that I didn't want to discuss it further.

He stared back at me, his gaze warm.

'We really should try and wake him up,' I said in a softer voice.

'My mom just throws water on me when I don't wake up,' he remarked.

We looked at each other and smiled.

'Papa, wake up,' I said, shaking his arm. He harrumphed in his sleep. 'Ma is going to be so embarrassed if she sees you sleeping here like this,' I said in a loud whisper.

Ma had looked over a couple of times and frowned when she saw Papa sleeping.

He mumbled something.

'What?'

'Wake me up when everyone is gone,' he said.

'No. That's not how you behave with people who have come to your party,' I protested.

I looked at Raghu for help and he nudged Papa.

'Uncle, wake up. Aunty isn't looking too well,' he said.

At this, Papa sat up as though he really had been doused in cold water. I glared at Raghu, but he shrugged. It had worked.

'Where? What happened?' he asked.

'She's all right,' I reassured him but the scare had been enough to wake him up.

I looked over at her then. She was sitting alone and she looked anxious and winced suddenly. I got up and went to her.

'What happened?' I asked.

Beads of sweat had popped up on her forehead but she smiled. 'Nothing. Just feeling a little warm.'

'Are you sure?' I persisted.

'Yes. It's not like I did anything. You guys did all the work,' she said. 'Has your father been sleeping?'

I looked back at Papa guiltily. Raghu was trying to make him eat something. 'Well, he sort of got bored . . .' I started.

'Let me guess. Then he had one drink too many and he dozed off,' Ma said wryly.

'Yeah. Something like that. Are you really okay?'

'Yes, yes. I'm all right. Once I eat some dessert, I'll be fine,' she added.

I rolled my eyes. 'Were you like this during the time you were pregnant with me too?'

Ma grinned. 'I don't remember those days very clearly. But this love for desserts . . . no. I would have remembered that.'

We talked some more and then I got up to get dessert for her. People started leaving soon after.

'Isn't it still quite early?' I asked her as she watched Ashwin leave.

'Well . . . partying in your forties is a lot different from partying in your twenties,' Ma quipped.

'And you would know that because . . .' I asked, grinning.

Ma, a party girl? That was Aunty V, who still looked like she could go on for another three or four hours, talking and laughing with people.

As I was looking at people saying their goodbyes, my gaze kept getting drawn back to Raghu, who was keeping Papa company. I was embarrassed at what I had told him today, about my struggles with my body.

What had gotten into me? Why would he care about all that? But what about those looks we'd been sharing? What did that mean? I didn't know how to define what had been going on between the two of us, except that I liked it a lot.

'Raghu cleans up well,' Ma commented and I looked away from him with a start. I knew what she meant. He wasn't exactly a slob, but he'd made an effort to look nice today.

When everyone had left, Ma got up to go inside. 'Shekhar, I need to talk to you,' she called out to Papa.

Aunty V, Raghu and I cleared up the debris of the party as best as we could. I was tired. This had been a long day.

'Veena!' Papa called out, as I was going inside. Something in his voice made me run, anxious with worry.

In the hall, Ma was sitting on the sofa, clutching her lower stomach, her face pale and sweaty.

'What happened?'

'My stomach. It's hurting,' she gasped. 'I think I'm bleeding.'

23

R aghu drove us to the hospital that night.

Papa had been drinking. He was mad at himself for being so irresponsible — having a pregnant woman in the house meant that anything could happen. I could see the self-recrimination on his face, but didn't say anything to him. He sat in front with Raghu and held his head in his hands.

In the back seat, Aunty V held Ma's hand while I held the other. Tears were streaming down her face.

I glanced at her stomach, my own tying up in knots. I used to be worried for Ma at first. But now . . . I was worried for the baby too. I put my palm on her stomach and was surprised when I felt a kick.

'Ma! The baby's kicking. It's going to be fine,' I said in a strangled voice, hoping I could convince her.

'See? Relax. Just relax. Don't let your BP shoot up,' Aunty V said soothingly.

Raghu pulled up in front of the emergency ward. We had called ahead and the hospital staff was waiting for us with a stretcher. Nurses helped Ma on to the stretcher and wheeled her away. I followed as far as I could, holding her hand until they took her to a separate room.

The four of us sat outside in a sombre line. I was terrified. I had no idea that things could get like this.

'She's going to be fine. The baby is going to be fine,' Aunty V said to no one in particular.

We sat there in silence. My stomach was churning. The worry on our faces must have been evident to anybody who saw us. Ma's gynaecologist was not there, but she was monitoring everything remotely, over the phone.

At long last, the doctor stepped out of the examining room where they had taken Ma.

Papa stood up, his face pale.

The doctor looked at us and smiled in a tired sort of way. The smile eased some of my worry.

'The baby's heartbeat is good. It should be fine. But just to rule out any issues, we're taking her to the ultrasound room now. She wants you all to come with her,' he said.

We got up in a rush and followed him. It was nearly midnight now and my body ached, but I tried to push it all to one corner so I could focus on Ma.

The orderlies wheeled Ma out and took her to the lift that would take them to the ultrasound room.

The lift could only fit in the stretcher, Papa, Aunty V, the doctor and the orderlies.

Raghu and I took the stairs. We ran up to join them as the lift doors opened and even though Raghu didn't say a word, I was glad of his company.

I finally got a good look at Ma. She was holding Papa's hand and still looked pale. Papa's expression was grave.

'What are we waiting for?' I asked, wanting to do something, the burst of energy and adrenaline inside me strong.

'The ultrasound doctor is coming now,' Aunty V said.

When the ultrasound doctor came and saw all of us, he looked displeased.

'Only the husband, please,' he muttered and walked away, but stopped when Ma called out to him.

'No, I want my family,' Ma insisted.

He looked annoyed. 'Who are all these people?' he asked.

'My family,' she said.

Shaking his head, the doctor opened the door and the orderly took her inside.

We crowded inside the small room as they shifted her to the bed near the machine.

'I think Mom and I should wait outside.' Raghu looked uncomfortable and anxious.

'Please stay,' I told him, suddenly needing him beside me.

The doctor applied some gel on Ma's exposed stomach and started rubbing the stick-like instrument over it. The black and white screen beside him sprang to life.

Papa moved forward and the doctor observed everything in silence at first. Then sighing, he beckoned us closer.

'See, that's the head,' he said, pointing at a spot on the screen.

I peered but couldn't see a thing. It looked like a few bubbles floating around.

'And those are the limbs,' he said.

I still couldn't understand anything.

'So from what I can see, everything is fine. The amniotic fluid is a little on the low side. The doctor will advise you on what to do,' he said, handing Ma a paper towel to wipe off her stomach.

Ma looked tired but better than she had been before. Papa had tears in his eyes.

'What advice?' I asked, my voice down to a whisper.

'That's how doctors talk,' Aunty V said. She looked drawn.

I looked at the tiny screen, at the blob-like image of my sibling that remained frozen on it and felt overwhelmed.

The doctor who had met us before came inside the ultrasound room. 'I only want one person in the room now. The rest of you can leave,' he said.

Reluctantly, all of us trailed out, except for Papa.

The first floor and the floors above were on a mezzanine floor that looked out over the central atrium. I walked up to the balustrade and Raghu joined me. Aunty V lingered near the door of the ultrasound room.

Papa emerged a little later, looking relieved. 'The gynaecologist has advised complete rest and wants Chitra to stay tonight for observation. Tomorrow, she's going to see her. They're preparing a room now.'

Aunty V burst into tears. Papa looked at her, shocked.

'I'm sorry. This is all my fault! I shouldn't have organized the stupid reunion party. All that stress and excitement did this to her.'

Raghu and I looked at each other for a moment before looking away quickly.

Papa was shaking his head. 'No, these things happen, V. It's nobody's fault,' he said, but I knew he probably blamed her a bit.

Aunty V shook her head. 'The three of you go home. I'll stay here with her tonight.'

'No, I'll stay,' Papa said.

They argued back and forth until Raghu intervened: 'I think we should all stay.'

'You should go back home and get some sleep,' Papa said to me and Raghu.

I shook my head. 'No, I want to be here with Ma.'

'Uncle, none of us are going to get any sleep if we go home anyway,' Raghu added.

I nodded. Aunty V looked conflicted, but she nodded too. 'They won't allow all of us to stay with her. We'll be with her in turns maybe. The rest of us can be in the waiting room.'

Ma was going to be in a room on the third floor. Raghu and I walked up the two flights of stairs slowly instead of waiting for the lift.

'Are you okay?' Raghu asked me as we reached the second floor landing.

'I guess. I was worried for a while though.'

'We all were. But I'm glad it's all fine,' he said.

We walked up the rest of the steps in silence. There were plenty of chairs in the waiting area, and there were three other people sitting there, dozing off. A flat-screen TV on the wall was playing Animal Planet without any sound.

We settled down—Raghu, Papa and I. Aunty V was in the room with Ma.

'They're fine. Both of them—Chitra and the baby,' Papa assured us, but it sounded like he was assuring himself.

When Ma had settled in, Papa went inside to talk to her.

'Get comfortable,' Raghu said, leaning back and stretching his arms over his head. He rolled his shoulders, easing off kinks.

'You should have gone home. You were going to sleep anyway, right?' I said, trying not to be look at the way his t-shirt was riding up, exposing his stomach.

'I'm glad I didn't go to sleep,' he muttered. 'Or Uncle might have forgotten that I can drive and he would have driven himself.'

I nodded solemnly, resolving to learn driving too.

We sat in silence for a while—a man in the room was snoring lightly. My fears about Ma and the baby were allayed and I was glad . . . no, *happy* to have Raghu with me.

As if he'd read my mind, Raghu spoke, eyes on the TV screen. 'I'm glad I'm here.'

'I'm glad too,' I said softly. He turned to me then, his gaze soft. There was that moment again, but this time, we were sitting close to each other. My lips parted. I wanted to say something but my mind had blanked out completely.

Why are you looking at me like that?

He would definitely ask, 'like what' and I wouldn't know what to say. It sucked that I couldn't articulate what I was feeling.

My heart thundered in my chest when, with a smile, he picked up my hand and squeezed it lightly. It was meant to be reassuring, but I couldn't help but wonder if Raghu was attracted to me. Did he see me as more than a friend? I wanted to ask him, but didn't want to sound presumptuous.

I let him hold my hand and I turned away to look at the TV screen. A cheetah was chasing a deer. I sensed him lean in closer.

'What are you doing?' I asked him finally, my voice a whisper, even as I continued staring at the TV screen. My stomach seemed to have dropped out of my body because of Raghu's nearness.

'Trying to figure out if your perfume smells better than your hair,' he said.

I turned to face him then, my throat feeling as if it was blocked.

I had to know.

'Are you flirting with me?' I asked him.

He looked embarrassed, but then he tightened his hold on my hand before letting it go.

'I don't know,' he said, not looking at me.

I wanted to shake him hard, but he'd withdrawn and I felt like I couldn't reach out to him. Why did I open my big mouth? Why couldn't I have kept quiet? I didn't know what to do. I was sure that if I said something now, I would reveal just how much I liked him. And then he would become even more uncomfortable and my extremely fragile self-esteem would get completely demolished.

I folded my arms across my chest and inched away from him. He sat beside me stiffly, his posture mirroring mine. Both of us were looking at the TV screen.

A lion was chasing a buffalo which turned around and tried to trample him. The lion sank his teeth into the buffalo's neck.

24

I woke up with a start. Where was I?

It came back in a rush — Ma, the hospital, the baby and . . . Raghu. I pushed my hair back from my face and stretched to ease out the knots in my neck — and realized I had fallen asleep on his shoulder. I straightened myself immediately and looked at him. He was asleep too. Thank god!

Heart still pounding, I checked the time. It was 3 a.m.

I got up slowly, my neck still hurting, and saw that Papa was sleeping on a chair nearby.

A nurse went inside Ma's room holding a machine and anxiety hit me hard. Was something wrong? I followed the nurse inside the room, my eyes adjusting to the light inside.

Ma and Aunty V were both awake. Ma was lying down. Aunty V appeared tired, but smiled at me and beckoned me with a nod. I sat down on the attendant's bed beside her, and watched the nurse hook up the machine to Ma.

'What's she doing?' I whispered.

'Wait and watch,' Aunty V whispered back. 'Or rather, listen.'

A loud dhub, dhub, dhub sound filled the air. It was strong, persistent and reassuring — the baby's heartbeat!

The nurse smiled, disconnected the machine and took it away.

'Why is she doing that at three in the morning?' I asked, my own heart beating loudly. I had just heard my sibling's heartbeat and suddenly, this person had become more real to me than when I had seen it on the ultrasound.

'They're monitoring the baby's heartbeat every hour,' Aunty V explained.

'And? Is it fine?' I asked, going closer to Ma.

Ma nodded with a weak smile.

'But you wouldn't have been able to sleep at all!'

'We'll sleep when we get back home,' Aunty V reassured me. 'Do you want to sleep here on the bed for a while? You guys should have gone home.'

I shook my head. But I didn't want to go back outside yet. Raghu was there.

Things were going to get weird between us. Why couldn't I have flirted back with him? Why on earth had I asked him that question? I'm so stupid, I told myself.

'Okay, I'll sleep here for a bit,' I said.

Aunty V got off the bed and stepped out. She switched off the lights on her way out.

'Ma?' I kept my voice low.

'Hmm?'

'Are you afraid?' I was hoping that she would say no. I needed her to be strong and invincible. Seeing her like this was taking everything out of me.

'A little,' she admitted.

I sat up and looked in her direction in the semi-darkness. 'Why?'

She sighed. 'We've still got another four months before the baby is born. So much could go wrong!'

I shook my head vehemently. 'No, it won't. It's going to be fine.'

'Just saying it won't make it happen, you know,' she replied. Her voice sounded as if she was tired but smiling.

'Ma, if you rest enough it's all going to be fine,' I told her. I was trying to convince both her and myself.

'I'm already resting,' she said, rolling her eyes. 'There are times when I can't wait for life to get back to normal.'

175

I had only thought about how much *my* life would change once the baby came. I had never considered how difficult it would be for Ma. My feelings over this baby had changed slowly—I was no longer embarrassed. All I wanted was for Ma to be okay and for the baby to be born without any hiccups.

I didn't want to say anything to her which would sound trite or clichéd, so I lay back down and shut my eyes. I went to sleep holding on to the dhub dhub sound I'd heard.

The next day, Ma was discharged after her doctor came to check on her. All of us probably looked like roadkill, especially since we had rushed over from the party. I avoided looking at Raghu.

Ma's doctor, a tall woman with short grey hair, said that she needed to be very careful. The pain was not good news and the bleeding was even worse. But it was going to be fine if Ma took all the precautions and rested well.

'Complete bed rest. Lying down. Not even sitting up,' the doctor told us all.

Ma looked at her, horrified. 'For how many days?' she asked in a strangled voice.

'At least the next ten days. We can't take chances, Chitra,' the doctor said sternly.

Ma wasn't even allowed to walk back to the car. She sat on a wheelchair and was wheeled out. Raghu offered to bring the car around. Papa nodded. His grip on Ma's file was tight and his knuckles were white.

When Raghu brought the car, Ma stepped down carefully and sat in the back. To my dismay, both Papa and Aunty V sat in the back with her, which left no option for me but to sit in the front.

Deciding not to agonize over it, I got in and pretended not to notice how sexy his arm looked when he changed gears. I was hopeless. All these days of pining after him and the one time he showed real interest in me, I'd blown it.

We drove home in silence. Raghu was extremely careful over the potholes which were scattered on almost all roads in Bangalore.

Aunty V helped Ma settle down in bed and we all went to our rooms to sleep.

I looked at myself in the mirror before I removed my dress. Something weird seemed to happen every time I wore it. The first time, there was the news about the baby. And now, the realization that this crush on Raghu was far worse than I had thought it was. And possibly not as one-sided as I'd thought.

25

When I relayed what happened to Nisha, she was really concerned about Ma. 'I hope Aunty's fine now,' she said.

After a while, we went on to talk about what had happened between me and Raghu. Anirudh was not in today and it was weird not to have him hanging around, but I was secretly pleased to have Nisha to myself for once.

'Ananya, *why* did you ask him if he was flirting with you?' she moaned.

I didn't know why I couldn't have just shut up instead of completely losing my cool.

'Never mind. Maybe he'll like your no-nonsense approach,' she said, trying to console me.

'Er, I don't think he did. He stopped talking after that.'

She sighed. 'Give it a little time. He probably needs to figure it out in his head too. Have you spoken to him after that?'

'I haven't seen him since we got home. We all went to sleep for a bit and when I woke up, he was out. He didn't come back home until I had gone to bed and when I left for college, he was still sleeping,' I said. It sounded like he was avoiding me, I thought wincing.

She looked at me with an astute look I was very used to. 'So, tell me the truth. Just how much do you like him?'

I looked away for a few seconds to compose myself and licked my dry lips. 'I like him a lot,' I said finally.

I thought back to the many different moments with him, the time we spent playing chess in the park, the few times I'd caught him looking at me and looking away quickly, the moments in the kitchen and during that party. During the horrible time in the hospital when I was worried about Ma, having him with me had helped defuse my tension tremendously.

Nisha smiled. 'I can't really tell you what to say to him or how to behave with him. Just be normal. Anyway, both of you are going to be busy now.'

I frowned. 'Why? He's busy, yes. But me?'

Nisha raised an eyebrow. My eyes widened in understanding.

'Oh shit. Our finals are starting in two weeks!'

I thought about all that was going on at home, and how Ma and Papa were worried about her and the baby. It was odd that I no longer felt any resentment towards this baby, even though it was taking all the attention away from me. Normally, my parents would have been after me to make sure I studied enough and would have pestered me to think about what I would do for my undergraduate degree. I was relieved at the reprieve.

'Why don't we focus on our exams for now? Then figure out things with Raghu eventually,' Nisha suggested.

Since the finals were so near, the lecturers were giving us old question papers to work out. Many students weren't even in class, although some continued to come diligently for the attendance.

Anirudh's record of a 100 per cent attendance had come down to a dangerous 79 percent, something that had shocked him. Nisha and I had barely scraped by, with 76 percent each.

Raghu hadn't messaged me since yesterday. I had been getting used to the fun banter, the memes he sent, and to hunting gifs to send him. Had I ruined all that by being so blunt? That was so unfair. When I said this to Nisha, she pursed her lips.

'So you message him then. Get back that thread of comfort you had with him,' she suggested.

I brightened at the prospect of reaching out to him. I didn't know why I hadn't already. I knew just what to send him. It took a little time to hunt down the exact gif. Nisha frowned when she saw it.

'Um, really? You want to send that?'

I nodded.

'We were up all night and the TV in the hospital waiting room was playing Animal Planet!' I told her, grinning.

'I still don't get it,' she said.

'Never mind. He will,' I told her and hit send.

We both watched as the gif filled the screen—a buffalo attacking a lion and then getting killed—on repeat.

'Gross,' Nisha muttered.

The single tick turned double and then turned blue. I held my breath, remembering that this scene had come on TV just after he'd been flirting with me. I hadn't mentioned that to Nisha.

I could see him online but there was no reply. As the seconds ticked by, I was regretting sending him the gif. I should have just said 'hi'. I put the phone on the desk, aware that I would have to hide it away as soon as the bell rang and the next lecturer came in.

'Come on,' I urged my phone silently.

Almost as though it had heard my silent plea, the screen lit up and I grabbed it.

He had sent a gif of Sridevi doing her famous nagin dance in her pink ghagra, twirling and hissing at the screen. It made me laugh loudly.

The phone lit up with another message.

'Let's be clear. I nagin, but you no sapera. You mongoose.'

The grin on my face refused to die down even when the lecturer walked inside the classroom briskly, holding her register.

26

I didn't meet Raghu that evening or the next. We texted once or twice, but I wanted to see him again, to gauge how things were between us. I discovered I'd have to wait for a very long time because the day after that, Aunty V informed me that Raghu had returned to Mumbai.

'Why?' I asked, surprised. I was disappointed that he hadn't even bothered to tell me he was leaving. Surely, he could have let me know.

'It's his father. He wants Raghu to study and take some tests for his university applications,' Aunty V replied, looking grim. She seemed to have forgotten that she had wanted him to do that too. Maybe seeing Raghu happy working at the restaurant had changed her mind.

What about what Raghu wanted, I wanted to know. I was surprised at how forlorn I felt at the thought of not meeting him again and not even knowing when he was coming back.

'Raghu is just doing it so that his father shuts up. But in the end that boy will do what he wants,' she said, as though reading my mind.

I didn't know what to say to that so I walked away, wondering if he would text me. But I didn't hear from him for several days.

I wasn't heartbroken, but I was disappointed. I'd expected better from him. I'd been ignoring him all these years but that was different. We had cleared our misunderstanding and we were friends again, weren't we?

On the last day of college, Nisha urged me to send him a selfie of us. We were both wearing pastel sarees for our farewell and we knew we looked great. The farewell should have been a big deal in college but so many were worried about the impending exams that many people skipped it. Anirudh had wanted to bunk too, but Nisha had convinced him otherwise. The guys were wearing suits and looked smart, but they weren't a patch on the girls. Nisha was wearing a peach-coloured saree and mine was pale blue.

I didn't think it was a great idea to send him a selfie. There had been radio silence from him for days now.

'But he'll think I *want* him to notice me,' I said, making a face.

'So? Let him think what he wants,' Nisha said with a shrug. 'You're looking so pretty today. He should realize what he's missing out on.'

As if, I thought, as I pushed my hair back. I'd cut it to shoulder length and got it styled for the farewell.

I thought back to the morning when Aunty V and Ma had helped me drape my saree. When they had finished, I'd stepped back and looked into the mirror in Ma's room, feeling different for the first time.

'So grown up you look,' Ma said, her eyes shiny.

I turned this way and then that. I couldn't see the usual bulges that made me wince whenever I saw my body in the mirror. Wearing the saree made me realize I actually had curves, which looked good.

'Sexy,' Aunty V said, with a wink.

I adjusted the pallu over my chest and rolled my eyes.

'She fills up that blouse far better than you ever did, Chitra!' Aunty V chortled.

I blushed, a little scandalized.

'Arrey!' Ma said, frowning.

'Arrey what? So your daughter has better boobs than you ever had, *even* with your pregnancy,' Aunty V continued.

I felt my ears become hot.

'Shush. She's still a kid.'

'She is not. And you know that as well as I do. But anyway, let's help her with the make-up,' Aunty V said, swiftly changing the subject.

'No! I don't need help with make-up!' I protested.

'But why?' Aunty V asked, her hands on her hips.

'Because you guys think make-up means make-up from the 90s!' I said with a shudder. I was sure she was going to pull out frosty pink lipstick to wear. Seriously, they should ban frosty pink lipsticks! They were yuck.

She'd looked at my favourite plum matte shade distastefully as I kept it on the dresser.

'We had these matte shades back in our time too. It made us look like corpses,' she said.

I rolled my eyes. 'That's because foundation in your time sucked,' I told her as I applied primer on my face.

It was her turn to roll her eyes.

'Aunty V, how's Raghu?' I asked her, the words slipping out. The fool had just gone silent and was ignoring me completely.

She didn't seem to find my question strange. 'He's tired. He wants to come back here, but his father won't let him.'

'What do you mean?' I asked alarmed.

'He wants him to study for GRE. He blames me for letting Raghu take it easy this year. Thinks I should have pushed him and not given him time to figure things out.'

'Well, it's important for Raghu to figure out what he wants,' I said, annoyed at his father.

She shrugged.

I had another disturbing thought. 'He won't force Raghu to go away abroad or something, no?'

'No, I too had wanted Raghu to go abroad for further studies,' she said. 'But . . .'

'But?' I prompted her, holding my breath.

'I can see how happy he is at the restaurant. I've been rethinking my plans for him. I want to ask him if he wants to do a hotel management course instead.'

That would be cool, I thought, as she walked away. Raghu would be doing what he loved. I felt happy and envious of him at the same time.

Now, I turned to Nisha.

'How about I just change my profile DP. He'll see it then,' I said.

She rolled her eyes. 'How's that going to help? *You'll* never know if he's seen it.'

I gave in to her reluctantly. We took some group photos and then a couple of selfies together. We sorted through them and I picked out the most flattering of them in which I was with Nisha and Anirudh. I had my arms around them and I was right in the middle, a wide smile on my face. It was a happy smile. It showed that I had a life here and friends who cared about me.

Before I could overthink it, I sent it to him.

He replied a little later with a thumbs-up emoji, which annoyed me. But what had I been expecting? I decided I wouldn't respond to him.

But later that night, he messaged me again. 'Sorry, was busy when you messaged. Looking at everything carefully now.'

I frowned. What was he looking at carefully? I sent him a question mark.

'All the messages I got earlier today,' he replied.

Oh, okay. From his many friends in Mumbai and probably his girlfriends and ugh . . . that lame selfie from me. Why had I listened to Nisha and sent it to him, I thought, shutting my eyes when my phone buzzed again.

'You guys looking good. What's the occasion?' he asked.

'Farewell in college,' I typed back.

He went silent after that. I kept looking at my phone until I fell asleep.

This continued over the next few weeks. He would send me a message or a joke and I would respond. Then he wouldn't reply for a day or two. There wasn't any flirtation whatsoever.

Whatever it was we had shared in Bangalore had run its course. I just had to accept it.

27

My exams were upon me before I even knew it.

I hadn't met Nisha or Anirudh apart from a half-hour quick catch-up over coffee the day we went to college to collect our hall tickets. No one spoke much. Everyone was worried about the impending exams and what it meant for our future. I'd pushed Raghu out of my mind for the moment.

On the day of the first exam, I woke up, my stomach twisting with nervousness. I had practised a couple of old exam papers and I felt somewhat ready. I had studied as well as I could and was glad that Raghu wasn't around being a big distraction. His mother was distracting enough already, as she made all the desserts Ma kept demanding. The fridge was like Kryptonite for me and I gave it a wide berth whenever I went into the kitchen.

Ma was now nearing the end of her second trimester and it was getting difficult for her to move around. After that scare the previous month, she had been taking it easy, but she was getting bored.

Papa got her a Kindle. When I left my room that morning, wishing my stomach would settle down and stop acting funny, I found her reading.

'All set?' she asked. She was lying down on the sofa.

'Sort of,' I told her as I sat down at the sofa and put on my shoes.

'Eat something and go?' she suggested.

'Wouldn't be a good idea today.' The very thought of food was going to make me puke.

'You're going to write an exam on an empty stomach?' she asked.

'Let's not start this now, Ma,' I told her, getting up.

But Aunty V caught me in the hall and dragged me to the dining room. She had apparently made a full breakfast for me.

Aloo paratha with yoghurt *and* French toast. And there was a fruit salad as well—chopped fruits generously covered with condensed milk. Aaargh!

'So what's it going to be. Sweet or savoury?' she asked.

Maybe I could escape if I told her I'd take some and go. I went to the kitchen, grabbed some foil and wrapped up a paratha in it.

'I'll eat it on the way,' I lied.

'Don't think I haven't noticed what's been going on all these days I've been here with you all,' she said quietly.

I frowned. Aunty V had chosen a fine time for a confrontation. 'Aunty V, can we talk about this when I come back?' I asked.

I was anxious about the exam, worry unspooling in my stomach. She nodded.

'I remember what you said about being a work in progress, Ananya,' she said as I kept the foil covered packet in my bag.

I looked up at her, surprised. 'What?'

'You thought I didn't understand what you meant.'

My face heated. I didn't know what to tell her.

She patted me gently on the arm, shaking her head. 'We're *all* works in progress,' she said.

I stared at her, licking my suddenly dry lips.

'Think of right now. This moment. You're as perfect as you can be,' she said.

I frowned. 'Easy for you to say.'

The words slipped out though I hadn't meant to engage with her. How would she know what it was like to be me? To endure what I'd endured.

She shook her head. 'It's not easy, Ananya. Never is,' she said.

I shook my head too, mirroring her action, needing to get away from there.

'I've got to go now,' I muttered and walked away.

When I got into the auto, I realized I was still clutching the aloo paratha. My stomach growled as though aware of the proximity of food. I had to deny it, of course. Maybe I'd give it to a kid on the street if I saw one. But all the signals were clear and I was near college already, still holding to the damn thing in my hand.

Maybe I could split the paratha with Nisha and ensure that she ate the most of it. I texted her, asking her to meet me just inside the gate. She replied saying she was already near the classroom.

Fine, I texted back, a little irritated. I glared at the paratha like everything was its fault.

The auto sputtered to a stop near the gate and paying the fare, I got down.

The atmosphere in college was strange. There was a silent frenzy — students doing last-minute feverish studying, exchanging various photocopied notes. My stomach clenched in worry.

I dumped the foil-wrapped paratha into my bag and went to the room where I had my exam. Nisha was not in the same room but Anirudh was.

Seeing all the nervous faces around me ratcheted up my anxiety. As I took a swig of water from my bottle, I spotted Anirudh, but didn't go up to him. He would rattle on about all that he had studied and that would just make me more nervous.

The room where Nisha was writing her exam was just adjacent to ours. I wandered over and found her going over her notes.

She looked at me and smiled, but went back to poring over her notes.

'All set?' she asked.

'I think so,' I told her, willing the acid in my stomach to stop rolling around.

'Here, have some of this,' she said.

I looked at her, amazed as she pulled out a packet of crackers and handed it to me. How had she known that I wouldn't have eaten anything and that this might be the best thing for me right now?

'Thanks,' I said as I ripped it open and pulled out one of the square dry crackers. My thoughts briefly went to the paratha lying at the bottom of my bag.

'Listen, it's just an exam. We'll do our best and see what happens,' she said nervously. It was like she was trying to convince herself.

I hated organic chemistry from the bottom of my heart. I suppose I could clear my confusion about what I wanted from my life by process of elimination and that would remove all the irritants like chemistry, physics and maths. I didn't mind biology, but I could hardly see a future in it.

'Yeah,' I told her, chewing the cracker and swallowing it with water. Some of the churning in my stomach settled.

'Don't drink too much water or you'll want to use the restroom in the middle of the exam. They might make a fuss about that,' she warned.

She was right. I picked up my textbook when my phone pinged. I knew we had to leave our phones with our bags outside the classroom. The bell would ring soon, but I had to see the message.

It was from Raghu. I stared at it in surprise. It wasn't a personal message though, as he had sent a gif of Spongebob Squarepants giving a thumbs-up sign with a 'good luck' banner on top.

I smiled and my heart raced a little. I put the phone away and went on to the room where I had to write my exam.

Three hours later, Anirudh and I emerged after the exam. I was feeling drained, my fingers cramping from all the writing we had to do.

'One down, five more to go,' I groaned.

'It will be over soon,' Anirudh said absently.

He spotted Nisha coming out of her room, eyes trained on him and the two of them met and hugged like they hadn't seen each other in days. I didn't roll my eyes at them but stood back a little, suddenly wanting what they had with each other.

The two of them broke apart quickly, Anirudh looking around a little self-consciously. People around us were busy discussing the question paper, something I didn't want to do at all.

'I'll see you two at the next exam,' I told them and walked away.

'Ananya, wait!' Nisha called out and ran up to me.

'Hey, it's cool. I have to go home anyway.' We hugged and then she smiled.

I realized I didn't resent her or Anirudh at all. I'd probably be doing the same if Raghu was studying here and . . . and if we were together.

28

On the way back, I debated if I should call him. We hadn't texted much in weeks, so I had been surprised to get the good luck message from him. Maybe Aunty V had told him about my exam. Maybe (I hoped) he'd asked her about me.

I suddenly wanted to hear his voice. So, before I could stop myself, I dialled his number.

He answered on the very first ring and I sat back in the auto, secretly feeling pleased.

'How was the exam?' he asked, surprise evident in his voice.

'Okay. Ish. Not sure,' I told him, aiming for light banter with my tone, even though my heart was once again racing. Shit. I still had it bad for him.

'Why?' His voice warm and friendly. But that was what it was. Friendly.

'I *hate* organic chem, man!' I said, injecting a note of forced frivolity in my tone.

'Ugh, me too. I'm so glad all that is behind me now.'

'So, I heard you're coming back to Bangalore?' I asked and wanted to slap my forehead at the same time. What on earth had prompted me to ask him that? Ugh. Stupid, fool, I berated myself.

There was a moment's silence. 'Why? Missing me?' he asked, a teasing note in his voice.

'As if! How is your GRE prep going?' I asked, hoping to change the topic.

'No clue. It's all so annoying. My father doesn't really listen to anything I say. He just steamrolls over my objections.' Raghu sounded bitter.

'But . . . but it's your life. He can't force you to do what you don't want to do.'

'Yeah, tell that to him.' I sensed the withdrawal in his tone, even as I realized how much I enjoyed listening to his voice.

'So when is the test?' I asked quietly.

'In a few weeks. I have to sit down with my mother and make her understand what I want to do in my life.'

I processed this in silence, remembering what Aunty V had said. Should I tell him? Should I make him feel like there was something to look forward to at the end of all this? Would it make him feel better? I decided to jump into it and worry later. I was sure he would be pleased to hear what Aunty V had been considering.

'Um, listen. Don't tell her that I said anything to you, but . . . Aunty V was saying that she might consider letting you do a hotel management course if you wanted to.'

The auto was stuck at a traffic signal and around us, there were cars and other vehicles waiting for the signal to change.

There was silence on the other end. I pressed my ear closer to my phone straining to hear him.

'You're joking, right?' he asked.

'No, she did tell me, but I don't know how serious she was,' I added quickly.

'You just made my day, Ananya!' he said, his voice excited. 'I love you, man!'

My face flushed at his words and I cleared my throat. He'd meant it in a different way. A way that didn't mean anything. But I had this warm toasty feeling inside me, something that reached down to the tips of my fingers and toes and I shut my eyes as the auto started once more.

He was clearly unaware of the import of his words because they obviously didn't mean anything to him.

I cleared my throat again. 'Hey, so don't tell her I said anything. Please.'

'I won't! I won't! But really, I'm so happy! I thought I'd have to really work at convincing her.

And this just makes my job easier. I can't wait to get back to Bangalore now and I have you to thank for that,' he said.

My face had turned warm again and I had to remind myself that Raghu probably didn't even remember flirting with me. I was just his friend. His fat friend. My heart sank at the harsh reminder.

'Ananya?' he said suddenly, making me realize I had zoned out.

'Hmm?' I blinked at the warmth in his voice and I pictured him, that easy smile on his face, his eyes crinkling at the edges.

'Thanks. Really.'

'No problem. I've got to go now,' I said and ended the call because I couldn't keep hearing his voice and not feel anything.

Calling him had been a mistake, I berated myself. I was feeling all sorts of things after hearing his voice. The 'I love you' he had said was what friends say to each other all the time, but my emotions were all over the place.

I took a deep breath and put my phone away. My hands curled around something crinkly and I frowned. What could it be? Then I remembered the aloo paratha from this morning. I pulled it out and unrolled a little of the foil from the top. It was cold and looked soggy but I bit into it anyway. It was still delicious. I thought back to Aunty V's words this morning.

Did she really think that I was perfect now, as I was? Was that possible? There was so much I had to do before I could allow myself to think of myself as 'normal', let alone perfect. I chewed the paratha slowly.

My phone pinged.

It was Aunty V. Odd that she would text me just as I was thinking of her. She didn't say anything in the text though. She had just shared a link. I frowned as I clicked on it, wondering what it could be. It was a link about something called body neutrality.

I scoffed at it as I scrolled down, not really reading anything. Rich of Aunty V to send me motivational stuff, I thought, annoyed. I hated hearing about body positivity. It annoyed the hell out of me because it was easy for everyone else to say things like love your body. They weren't me. They didn't know how I felt. Why should I love my stupid body if I didn't want to?

I still glanced down the article and one sentence in particular popped out at me.

How I feel about myself has nothing to do with my appearance.

What? That was absurd. It had *everything* to do with my body, I thought as I wrapped up the rest of the paratha and stuffed it back inside my bag, feeling a sudden burst of anger, the warm feelings from my conversation with Raghu all but forgotten.

29

E ven though we stayed in the same house, Aunty
V had started sending me texts. She kept out of
my way because I was studying, but I was glad
because I didn't want to 'discuss' the things she'd
been sending me. Most of the time, I deleted the links
without opening them, but sometimes, curiosity got
the better of me and I read a couple of them.

The ideas confounded me, and despite not
wanting to, I found myself getting drawn into some
of them. I read and re-read one particular sentence
by someone called Alison Stone, a psychotherapist:
'When we spend less time thinking about our bodies,
it affords us room to focus on other things.'

Could it be true, I wondered. What did it mean
for me?

There were also some famous actresses who were
talking about how they didn't want to spend time
looking at themselves in the mirror because they had

so many other wonderful things to do. I frowned because it was easy for *them* to say that. *They* were gorgeous. But if I were to understand this concept, it wasn't about looking in the mirror and finding good things about myself. It was about looking at my body and thinking of what it allowed me to do, about my body as a functional being, not as an object to be admired.

I put away my phone and tried to focus on my studies, but the words from other women, not just celebrities who felt this way, kept floating back into my mind. Was it possible? If I didn't have to love my body, I didn't have to hate it either? What of Ms Piggy and Fat Ananya, I wondered. The words that had scarred my mind and shaped my life. I had allowed them to become alternate personas. But what if I was able to treat them just as words? What if I stopped giving them so much importance? Was it even in my control?

I was sure that if I were to meet Esha today, she'd still have unflattering things to say about the way I looked, especially my body. But why did she have that sort of power over me? Because I gave it to her. I frowned. There was no way Esha was going to have any sort of power over me. I wasn't going to let her. I was no pushover.

I decided to think about this more, after my exams, when my phone pinged.

It was Raghu, sending me a meme that had Jon Snow crying, the heading at the top reading, 'Me after studying for 1067 hours' and the caption below, saying, 'I do know some things.'

I grinned.

Both mother and son were monopolizing my texting time all of a sudden, because after our chat on the phone, Raghu had started sending me texts every day.

I still spent an unnecessary amount of time over them, mulling over my replies. Sometimes I hunted down the right memes to send back, sometimes I would let it be because it became too exhausting to be clever and funny all the time. I figured he wasn't holding his breath, waiting for me to reply. I felt sad that I had crossed over into the friend zone.

There were many times when I just wanted to come right out and ask him if he was single, if he was seeing someone in Mumbai, but I stopped myself. The messages we shared were almost generic. I couldn't pop in with a personal question casually. At the same time, I felt maybe there wasn't anyone or he would have mentioned it. I couldn't be sure.

And this wasn't something that I could ask Aunty V. She was very shrewd and I was trying to avoid direct discussions with her because I didn't want to end up talking about my body issues.

So we continued this way, texting on and off. And soon my exams were over and I was a free bird.

I was glad to be home, but beginning to worry about what I would do once the results were out. The admission forms for various colleges were already available on their websites. I would have to make a decision soon.

I knew I wasn't cut out for a professional course like medicine or engineering or even architecture, like Nisha. That left me with the usual humanities and commerce streams if I wanted to escape science, especially organic chemistry.

I sat at my desk one morning, when everyone was still asleep, writing down the different options I had. As usual, I was torn — glad that my parents were so busy with the baby, and hadn't started hounding me about what I wanted to do with my life, but also slightly resentful that the baby had managed to eclipse my needs at this hour.

When I looked at Ma, I felt awful. There was no place for any resentment. She was nearly eight months pregnant and getting bigger by the day. She had more than a hundred aches and pains and her feet were constantly swollen. I couldn't blame *her* for not focusing on me. She had too much going on. But Papa?

I made a face when I thought of him and ruled out B. Com from my list of courses. I was certainly not going to spend three years of my life studying commerce and accounts. And this decision left me with even fewer choices.

I looked at the different combinations that were offered under humanities and while some were interesting, I didn't know if I would be able to sustain interest in it for more than a year. I needed to do something that I was passionate about and right now, I didn't know what that would be.

I dropped my pencil on the desk, thinking about how I needed to sort this when my phone buzzed.

It was a message from Raghu. I looked at it surprised. He never messaged this early.

'Wassup?'

Normally, I'd have replied back with the shrugging emoji, but I wanted to talk to him. He'd been so confused himself after his board exams last year. Surely, he'd have some idea of the turmoil and could help me. I asked if he was free to talk.

He called immediately. I answered, surprised, my heart still fluttering. We talked casually about my exams and a minute into the conversation, I realized that my voice became different when talking to him. It had that same high, breathy quality that Ma's voice had when she'd been speaking to ear-hair uncle at the reunion party.

That flustered me a little and I cleared my throat. 'So what's up?' he asked.

I told him about my dilemma and he listened in silence.

'So you don't want to do a humanities course?' he asked, sounding confused.

'I don't know. I don't feel like studying economics or history,' I told him.

'They do have literature and journalism,' he suggested.

'Not too keen on those either,' I told him.

'What do *you* want to do?' he asked.

'I don't know. I wish I knew. I wish we had time to decide what we wanted instead of rushing into the next thing.'

There was a moment's silence and then he sighed. 'That's why I took a break. To figure out what I wanted.'

'You're *right*! Everyone should do that. Take a gap year to figure out what they want,' I said, exclaiming loudly.

'Err, are you sure about this? Your parents may not be too happy about it,' he said, sounding worried. 'You know how much my mother went on about me taking a break. And my father . . . '

'My parents aren't too concerned right now,' the words slipped out before I realized what I was saying.

'Really?' he sounded surprised.

'No, I meant . . . they're just worried with the baby coming and everything. They've left this to me. So maybe I'll take some time to decide what I want too!' The plan made me feel relieved and a little anxious at the same time. I wasn't sure how they would take it when I told them that I wanted to take a year off like Raghu had done.

'Hey, listen. Um, you should make this decision *after* talking to them. I don't want Aunty and Uncle to blame me for putting the idea into your head.'

'No, don't worry. I won't bring you into it,' I assured him.

'Okay, but remember, a gap year isn't just for taking off time. You have to use that time to figure out all your shit.'

'Like you did?' I asked, feeling a little curious, a little sad that I'd distanced myself so much from him these past few years, I had no clue what had been going on with him.

'Yeah. It took me a while, but I did. And until I started working in that restaurant in Bangalore, I hadn't really understood how *much* I wanted to do this,' he said. I could sense the smile in his voice.

'That's nice. I'm happy for you, Raghu,' I said, feeling genuinely happy him, and for people like Nisha and Anirudh who knew what they wanted from their lives.

'Thanks,' he said. He added, 'I can't wait to see you . . . guys. Soon.'

My heart squeezed in my chest. For a second there, it had almost sounded like he said he couldn't wait to see *me*.

'Me too,' I replied because he was waiting for me to speak.

I glanced up at the calendar that hung on my wall as we said our byes and ended the call.

I couldn't wait for him to get back, even though I kept reminding myself of how he'd frozen up when I'd asked if he was flirting with me. He needn't know that he was way too special to be *just* my friend.

30

I got 82 per cent, which was neither here nor there. College cut offs for B. Com were all above 95 per cent, so I was grateful that was not what I had wanted to do.

I sat down with my parents and spoke to them about my plans for taking a gap year.

I sat on their bed and told them that I couldn't make up my mind. That I needed more time to figure out what I wanted to do.

'So you're telling us *now*? But how can you waste your time like this?' Ma asked.

'I'm not wasting my time, Ma. I want to be sure about what I'm doing. I don't want to rush into something just because everyone else is doing it.'

I caught Ma and Papa exchange a look between them.

'And what if you don't figure it out even then?' Ma asked.

'I need to at least try. Give myself the option.'

'Have you been speaking to Raghu about this?' Papa asked suddenly.

My face flushed at the mention of his name. 'We talked,' I admitted. 'And it makes sense.'

They were silent. Ma finally sighed. 'I feel like I let the ball slip on this because of the pregnancy. At least you should have followed up with her, Shekhar,' she told Papa, who looked away guiltily.

'No, it's okay. I'm glad you two weren't after me to get admission in some random course.'

'You children these days are too entitled. We just did whatever course we could get into and figured out what we wanted along the way,' Papa huffed.

Ma rolled her eyes at him. 'Just because it worked for us or because *we* did it doesn't mean it has to work for everyone.'

'Times are different, Papa. You always knew I wasn't going to get into a professional course. So just let me figure this out,' I said. 'Maybe I'll do a course or a diploma during this time. So it won't be a complete waste.'

Papa looked thoughtful. 'What about your friends? How have they performed?'

Well, Anirudh hadn't topped the state as he'd been hoping to and his parents were probably scratching their heads, wondering where he had gone wrong. But he had scored 96 per cent and had been moping around until Nisha knocked some sense into him. She had got 88 per cent and the two of them were going to be busy preparing for various entrance exams. I was going to meet them right after this conversation.

'They've done well,' I said, with a tight smile.

My parents were silent as they looked at me. I could sense the judgment rolling off them.

'Listen, it's going to be fine. Shouldn't my happiness be important to you guys?' I asked.

'But are you?' Ma asked me. 'Are you happy?'

I shrugged. 'I feel like even if it takes time to understand what I want to do, it's worth it. I don't want to do some random course just because I have nothing better to do.'

'Well, if this does make you happy, go ahead,' Ma said, sighing. 'But you're getting into a college next year, young lady, whether or not you figure out what you want.'

'And do what?' I asked, surprised.

'Whatever. Any course that interests you the slightest bit. You can't just take all your time to figure out what you want.' I spotted the old Ma in her tone and expression.

'If I remember correctly, you told Aunty V that it's all right if Raghu wants to take some time to figure out what he wants,' I reminded her.

Her face paled when she remembered her words. 'You know what? You kids *are* entitled,' she said.

I grinned as I got up, feeling a little better that they hadn't taken the news too badly. I met Aunty V who was on the phone outside and she smiled at me as she finished her call. She had been talking to Raghu.

'I've booked his ticket for the next weekend,' she told me.

Raghu would be here soon! I think the smile on my face was too wide, so I dialled it down a bit.

'Are you going somewhere?' she asked.

I nodded. I had made plans to meet Nisha and Anirudh.

'Come sit for a little while with me?' she suggested.

Oh no. I didn't want to sit and talk to her about the links she'd been sharing with me. I think she noticed the panic on my face, but she smiled grimly.

'Just a few minutes please?' she said.

'Uh, why?' I blurted out.

She didn't answer as she led me to the living room where we both sat down. She was uncomfortable too, I could tell. She cleared her throat.

'So, I've been sending you a few things to read these past few days,' she began. She looked nervous and took a deep breath.

I made a face, but didn't say anything.

She looked down at the carpet. 'The world was a very different place when we were young, Ananya,' she said.

I nodded, because what was I to say to that.

'In our days, our parents often body shamed us, made us feel inadequate, made us feel like shit if we didn't fit a certain idea of what we were supposed to look like.'

What?

'Surely not all parents?' I said.

'Of course, not all. But my mother and your nani were definitely guilty of that. My mom would go on and on about how I was too short and she made me feel terrible. I don't think she meant to, of course, but I was there in front of her and it was easy for her. As for your nani, she would keep comparing Chitra to a stick, saying she needed to put on weight,' she said.

I frowned. Aunty V and Ma were not childhood friends but they were close enough to have shared their traumas growing up.

'Chitra was a regular kid but your nani kept going at her constantly, saying she was doing this for her own good, that she wouldn't get a good match if she continued to be so thin. Now your Ma and I didn't let it affect us that much. We listened to them and we ignored them. It was easier and we were honestly having far too much fun in our lives,' she said.

'Why are you telling me all this?' I asked her finally.

'Because we didn't want to do that to our kids. We didn't want to make them feel inadequate. We wanted you all to feel loved. No matter what. And I'm telling you this now because I want you to be happy with yourself. I haven't had the chance to stay with you guys in a long time so I didn't notice before, but now that I'm here, I've seen how little you eat, and what you eat. It's not healthy, Ananya. Chitra told me some years ago that there was a period when you weren't eating anything at all. And she was worried about you. That she even took you to a psychiatrist.'

I looked down. 'Yeah, but I'm fine. I don't need any help,' I mumbled.

Aunty V shook her head. 'I would have brought it up with Chitra if she wasn't so tired and worried about having a baby in her forties, but I'm like your mother too. That's why I'm talking about this with you directly. You're a growing girl. You *can't* starve yourself to look a certain way,' she said.

'I'm not starving myself,' I protested. 'Do you think I'd still look like this if I was starving myself?' I extended my arms out without a thought and then brought them back in, closer to my body, my face turning red as I realized what I'd said.

She shook her head. 'Yes, you're not starving yourself, but I can't forget what you said about being a work in progress. *No one* is perfect. But you can't just keep striving to reach that certain level of perfection. You can't miss out on all the exciting things life has to offer because you're too worried about what you look like!'

I pursed my lips. I was getting tired of listening to her sanctimonious speech and of the body neutrality or positivity articles she kept sending me.

I shook my head. 'That's what you think, Aunty. But I won't be included in any of these "exciting things that life has to offer" unless I look a certain way. You can't be so naïve!' I said, getting up.

'No, wait, Ananya. It's not like that. Your confidence is in your mind,' she said, getting up too.

'Aunty V, please. When I was twelve, a thin and pretty girl called me a "fat bitch", "ugly cow" and "Ms Piggy" because of the way I looked. Don't tell me that the confidence in my mind could have shut it down,' I snapped at her.

Aunty V's face paled. 'Who . . .' she trailed off, because I was shaking my head.

'It's not important. I have to go now,' I said, and walked away to my room.

I was breathing heavily, my mind crowded with thoughts. Despite my anger at her, I realized that she was trying to help. She was trying to make me see my body and not cringe. To make me understand that my body was not my enemy. Was it working? I didn't know.

As I changed my clothes, I paused in front of the mirror.

Fat bitch, the voice whispered in my head again.

'Ya, so what?' I snapped at it viciously.

I stepped away from the mirror and the voices faded. I dressed quickly because I had received a couple of texts from Nisha, asking where I was.

By the time I reached the coffee shop, my anger had cooled off, but Aunty V's words still played on my mind. I pushed open the door and saw the two of them talking to each other intently. I felt that second-long moment of resentment, which I buried as I joined them.

They both got up to hug me and sat down and continued talking about something exam-related. When they realized I wasn't joining in, they stopped and turned to me.

'What's going on?' Nisha asked, reaching out and squeezing my hand.

I told them my plans of taking a gap year. Anirudh was aghast, as expected, but even Nisha looked shocked.

'But you'll be a year behind all of us!' she protested.

'It's not like we're going to be in the same class or college, so how does it matter?' I asked her.

'That's true. But . . . I don't feel too good about this,' she said, frowning.

Anirudh kept shaking his head, as though still in shock. 'This Raghu fellow has really messed with your mind,' he said finally.

I shot a look at him and sighed. 'Stop being such a thatha, Anirudh. He didn't say anything. I just realized this is what made sense for *me*,' I told them.

Anirudh made a face as he always did whenever I called him a grandfather. 'Of course he doesn't *need* to say anything. You're just following in his footsteps,' he said, as though it was obvious.

'I'm not,' I said crossly. 'And even if I were, it's fine. I'm just taking time out to decide what I want. What's wrong with that?'

This day was turning out to be way too much for me. First convincing Ma and Papa, then Aunty V's talk that had managed to rankle but rang with truth somehow, and now Anirudh's over the top reaction.

'Listen, one year is not going to make a difference in my life,' I told him.

Anirudh's eyebrows went up and he nodded in a most annoying way. 'Yeah, sure. That's because you're one of the lucky ones,' he said.

'Lucky?' I was surprised.

'Not knowing what you want is also a privilege, you know,' he said quietly.

I wanted to say something but he continued speaking.

'My parents have worked really, really hard to make sure I get admission at a medical college. I don't have the luxury of waiting around and figuring out what I want,' he said.

Nisha and I stared at him. 'But you also want it, right? You've always wanted it, no? To be a doctor?' Nisha asked.

Anirudh's words made sense to me suddenly. He didn't have a choice, whereas I had one. And then I realized that we had choices for most things and that made us lucky, just like Anirudh said. In the same way, I could *choose* to not hate myself. I had always had the choice. I just didn't know. I remembered Aunty V's words to me again.

Unaware of the epiphany in my head, Anirudh nodded. 'Yes, I do. But it would have been nice if everything didn't pile up together like this, if all of this weren't a race,' he burst out.

Nisha squeezed his hand and I smiled at him sadly. I recognized the truth in his words, that taking time off was a luxury and a privilege and I had to make sure I didn't misuse it.

31

In the ninth month of her pregnancy, Ma had appointments with her doctor every week. I went with her most times and it was painful to see her in so much discomfort.

On the last visit, the gynaecologist had said that everything was fine and the baby could make its appearance any day. That thought terrified me. Were we ready? Was Ma ready? But Ma seemed relieved. Of course she was ready. She had been waiting for nine long months! My appreciation towards what mothers went through had gone up several notches during her pregnancy.

Raghu was finally coming back. His flight was in the evening but by the time he'd get home, it would be quite late.

I tried to behave normally even though I was all jumpity-jump inside. I was awake watching a show on Netflix, while Ma was lying down on the sofa, watching the show with me.

I was keeping Ma company because she wasn't sleepy, or so she claimed. Since she slept so much during the day, sometimes she was awake at odd hours and usually she got hold of either Aunty V or Papa to hang out with her. Papa had a late business meeting and Aunty V was suffering from menstrual cramps, so she had gone off to lie down for a bit.

'Why is it that women get menstrual cramps even in their forties?' I asked Ma. 'Shouldn't that stuff be over by now?'

Ma paused the TV. 'Nothing really changes as you grow older, Ananya. If anything, it all just gets worse.'

Wow. Lead me down the dark path, Ma, I thought, but didn't say anything to her.

Aunty V and I hadn't talked again, but every time I saw her, she smiled at me. There was a look of empathy on her face that, for some reason, made it a little easier to look at myself in the mirror without cringing. She didn't stop sending links, but I didn't delete them. I opened and read every one of them. The words were soothing. The outcome was possible. The stories made me want to believe, even as I struggled with it.

The episode we were watching ended. The next one was about to start when Raghu came in. Papa had given him a key when he was here the last time.

My chest contracted and it felt like my heart had skipped a beat. I glanced at him, my mouth dry, and looked away just as quickly before our eyes could connect.

He looked tired and his face was drawn. 'Hi!' he addressed no one in particular.

'Hey, so nice to see you, Raghu. How have you been?' Ma asked, her face brightening up.

I looked up at him then because it was getting too difficult to not look at him. It was like there was something magnetic about him pulling my gaze towards his, and then I realized that he was looking at me too.

He smiled and I smiled back.

I looked down at my feet, wishing I'd bothered to change into something nicer. But why? We were just friends, right? And Ma would have wondered why I was taking trouble over my appearance, this late in the night.

'I've been good. Tired of studying. Don't want to look at another book now. Where's Mom?' he asked.

'Lying down in bed. Not well,' Ma said, almost apologetically. 'Come join us? Unless of course you're tired, which I'm guessing you must be. What about something to eat?'

He shrugged. 'I'm cool. Give me fifteen minutes. I'll take a shower and come back and maybe grab something to eat from the kitchen,' he said and walked off to the room he was sharing with Aunty V.

I watched his retreating back, feeling all sorts of emotions, very keenly. How was I going to hide it from him?

'I'm so glad they're both here,' Ma said.

I turned to her, trying to keep my expression neutral as I nodded. An idea was slowly forming in my mind. I'd been dying to know all these days if he was single or not.

'I wonder if his girlfriend is pissed at him for coming to Bangalore indefinitely,' I said, hoping my gambit would work.

Ma frowned. 'What girlfriend? Does he have one?'

I shrugged. 'I don't know. I guess?' But maybe now, Ma would ask him or Aunty V and I could listen in surreptitiously, I thought. This was a little devious but I was desperate to know the truth.

Ma kept frowning, thinking for a few minutes.

'Why are you so upset?' I asked her, wondering if I had done the right thing in bringing this up with Ma.

'I just never thought of that. I still think of him . . . even you . . . as small kids. If he did leave a girlfriend behind and . . .'

'Ma, you're behaving like he went to war or something,' I snapped at her, a little annoyed now.

'Yes, but if he *had* a girlfriend . . .'

'What girlfriend?' Raghu's firm voice interrupted Ma.

He looked squeaky clean after his shower and he was wearing shorts and that same pink vest I'd seen him wear so many times. But this time, the fluttering in my belly increased as he rounded the sofa and came to sit down. Since Ma was lying down on the long couch, he took the other single sofa near mine.

My stomach felt like it had caved in on itself. Stupid, stupid, I told myself in my head, not looking at him.

'*Your* girlfriend,' Ma said, wincing as she turned a little to look at him.

'Are you okay?' I found myself asking her even though I was desperate to hear Raghu's answer.

'I'm all right. These little aches and pains are going to be there until the baby comes,' she smiled. 'Raghu, I asked you something.'

'Yeah what about her?' he asked.

I tried hard not to look at him—so much so that my neck was straining with the effort. There *was* a her? There was *someone*? My heart sank. I wanted to get up and go to my room, but it would look odd so I stayed put.

'Was she upset about you coming away to Bangalore for so many days? And now that you're here again?' Ma asked.

I wished I'd never broached this subject. Who was she, I wondered suddenly. Was she slender and tall and had long hair like Esha? *Obviously. Raghu would have gone for that type*, I thought bitterly.

I almost didn't hear him speak then as he replied to Ma. 'Understatement of the century,' he said, rolling his eyes.

I couldn't help myself from looking at him.

'Why?' I asked him, despite wanting to shut up.

'What do you mean why? Because I was going to be away for so many days!' he said, looking earnestly at me.

I had to look away from his gaze, not sure how I was going to deal with this devastating news.

'Oh no! I'm so sorry! I never really thought of that when I demanded that V come and stay here with me,' Ma said, looking distraught.

I turned back to him, feeling agitated. 'You shouldn't have come here, then!'

If he had a girlfriend, why hadn't he said anything before? Why had he kept looking at me like that, and what was that flirting in the hospital?

He shrugged.

'It's okay. She understands now,' he said.

The three of us sat in silence for a few seconds. I didn't know what to think. Disappointment bloomed in my chest.

I looked at him—he was busy fiddling with his phone.

'Texting her?' I asked.

'Yeah. Problem?' he asked, without looking up from the phone.

I looked away and switched the TV off. 'I'm going to sleep,' I said.

Ma got up gingerly. 'I'll also go. It's quite late,' she said.

'But you guys asked me to join you two and now you're both off! Not fair,' Raghu complained.

I bit down on a retort, saying his girlfriend could keep him company. I didn't want him to know how insanely jealous I was.

'Sorry, beta. Maybe some other time. Eat something before you go to sleep,' Ma said as she walked towards her room slowly.

I got up and started walking away too when I heard him humming something and I stopped.

'Decided to stay back?' he asked, with a smile on his face, even though his gaze was still on his phone.

'What were you humming just now?'

He looked up and grinned. 'Guess?' he asked. His eyes glinted mischievously. The old Raghu, the one who pulled my leg every now and then, was back and it made me happy.

Everything just clicked into place.

I picked up the nearest cushion and started hitting him with it while he tried to protect himself by crossing his arms in front of his face as he laughed. I had heard right—and I was laughing too.

He had been humming the old Sridevi song 'Main Nagin Tu Sapera'.

Suddenly, he caught hold of my wrist and yanked me down. I toppled on top of him gracelessly. I dropped the cushion and my breath seemed trapped in my throat. No one was laughing any more.

He looked at me intently and then pushed away my hair from my face, gently, in a way that made my heart race.

'You could have just asked,' he whispered.

I felt hot, being so close to him. It was like he was burning me up.

'Asked what?' I whispered back. My heart was pounding so hard, I was sure he could hear it too.

'If I had a girlfriend,' he said.

'Do you?' I asked finally.

He smiled and shook his head.

I looked up at him again when he tightened his arm around me and brought me closer to him. I could feel the way his chest rose and fell. More than anything else, I was glad he was here. Glad he didn't have a girlfriend back in Mumbai.

'I've been waiting to see you all these days, Ananya,' he said softly.

I was suddenly conscious of myself, the way I was sprawled over him. I was heavy but he didn't seem to be bothered by that at all. I licked my lips nervously and his gaze was drawn there.

'Why?' I asked him. I wish I didn't have to ask this, that I wasn't desperate for validation.

He frowned. 'Because I like you?' he said. Why did he sound doubtful, like he wasn't sure himself?

'But why?' I persisted, shutting my eyes briefly. I was not glamourous, just passably pretty when I made the effort, and I was still not thin. Why would someone like Raghu like *me*? I needed to hear it.

'Because you're my friend,' he said and I wanted to facepalm so badly. I tried to keep my face impassive, but I obviously failed because a tiny furrow came up between his eyebrows.

'You're mad at me. I don't understand,' he said, looking anxious.

'You like me because I'm your *friend*?' I asked, quieting my flustered nerves.

'But . . .'

I took a deep breath. 'I like you too, but more than just a friend,' I said, shutting my eyes tightly, very briefly. There. I'd done it.

'Of course I like you as more than a friend too!' he said quickly.

I tried to sit up, but it wasn't easy.

'Yes, but you didn't say why,' I said, exasperated. 'Raghu, I don't want you being passive in this and . . .'

I stopped talking because he was looking at me, confused. He took a deep breath and tightened his hold around my waist. I was aware of my shallow breaths, of the just-appearing stubble on his face, but his words brought me back to my senses.

'So you want me to be aggressive?' he asked.

Idiot, I thought. The opposite of passive was not aggressive. I shook my head.

'I want . . .' he cut off my words when he held my face in his palms and lowered his head to kiss me.

32

I was shocked. Shocked that this was happening with Raghu.

It quickly turned into amazement when I realized how much I'd wanted this too. I kissed him back and it was everything and even better than anything I'd read in books or seen on TV. It was like Raghu and I just knew how to do this.

Probably because he had a lot of practice, I thought and I pushed him away, breathing heavily.

We looked at each other and I knew from his expression that he wanted to do it again, just like I did.

I put my hand on his chest. His heart was racing and I just used that excuse to feel his chest a little more with my palm. He caught my hand, looking at me intently.

'Was that you being aggressive?' I asked him softly. He didn't say anything, so I shook my head. 'I don't want you to be aggressive.'

'What *do* you want?' he said, pushing his fingers through his hair in a frustrated manner.

'You,' I said, not sure where the courage came from. His eyes lit up and he leaned close to kiss me again, but I stopped him.

'It's important to me that you want me too,' I said quickly.

'I wouldn't be doing this if I didn't,' he said, tracing my jawline with his finger.

'So this isn't just a novelty to you?' I persisted.

'Why would you say such a thing?' he asked, looking puzzled.

I looked down, not sure how I could explain my lack of self-esteem and what it meant to me to have him look at me like this. Like I was desirable and beautiful. But I couldn't say it without sounding pathetic. I wanted him to say the words to me but I couldn't spell out why I wanted him to. I squirmed at the way he was looking at me.

'So what happens after this?' I asked, belatedly realizing that it would sound sexually suggestive.

'Um . . .' he said, trying hard not to smile.

I covered my eyes with my palm in mortification and he peeled it away gently. 'I know what you meant,' he said, kissing my palm.

'And?' I said.

'And let's just take this a day at a time? See how it goes? I really, really like you, Ananya, but the truth is that I've *always* liked you. I've liked you best. You were my best friend even though we never lived in the same city. Even though we never met that often. Because whenever we met, we could just pick up from where we left off last time. I've never had that with anyone else. I don't make friends easily. But you, you've *always* been my friend, except that you're a friend I'm crazily attracted to now,' he said.

I don't know what warmed me more. His words or the earnest expression in his eyes, or his wandering hands that were running over my arms.

'One day at a time,' I repeated, feeling so happy inside that I could burst. I could take things one day at a time.

I leaned forward and took him by surprise by kissing him. That same thing flared between us and I knew then, that whatever happened between us later, this moment was always going to be special.

He felt wonderful as he kissed me back, his lips exploring mine and his hands running over my back. I snuggled closer to him and it felt amazing.

But anyone could come in and see us and I wasn't quite ready for that. Reluctantly, I pulled back and got up from the sofa. He got up too. He looked disappointed but understanding.

'I'd better go to my room,' I said.

'No, stay,' he said quickly.

I shook my head. 'Papa could come home any time now,' I reminded him.

'So? We'll just be two people sitting together and watching TV,' he said.

'Really? You think he won't be able to read what happened on our faces?' I asked him wryly.

'I hope not!' he said, eyes widening.

'Still, I don't want to give them anything to work with at the moment,' I said.

Raghu stood up, held my shoulders and tugged me closer. I put my arms around his waist. It felt good, so good, it was like something had opened up in my heart and spread the warmth through my body.

'This isn't a friendly hug, FYI,' he said.

I looked up at him. He raised an eyebrow.

'Which makes it all the more important that I go back to my room now,' I whispered.

'Fine,' he said reluctantly, letting go of me.

I was not really in the mood to go back to my room after this delicious moment, but I knew that the longer I prolonged it, the harder it would be.

'Good night,' I told him, leaning up and kissing him swiftly before I walked away.

I turned to look back at the end of the corridor and saw that he still looked surprised as he grinned at me. I winked and walked into my room, wondering if I had ever felt this happy before.

I shut the door and twirled. I called up Nisha and only when she answered groggily did I realize that it was late. But I had to tell her. I simply had to.

'Raghu and I kissed,' I told her in a loud whisper.

'What?' she mumbled.

I debated hanging up, but I wouldn't be able to sleep without talking about this with her.

'I said,' I enunciated slowly, 'Raghu and I kissed.'

'WHAT?' she shrieked.

I put the phone away from my ear briefly before bringing it back to my ear. 'I think my eardrums split.'

'But this was eardrum-split-worthy!' she continued in the same excited voice. 'What happened? How did this happen?'

I told her everything and she listened in silence. Complete silence.

'What?' I asked her, feeling uneasy for the first time that night. Since the moment Raghu had kissed me, I had been floating on a bed made of balloons.

'No . . . nothing, it's great,' she said, her tone suggesting that it was anything but great.

'Nisha, tell me,' I said.

'You didn't ask him why he ignored you when he went back to Mumbai? Or why he didn't even tell you he was going?' she asked.

It hadn't occurred to me at all. But did it matter now that we were together?

'Of course it matters,' she insisted. 'He has to communicate with you. He can't just suddenly up and leave whenever he wants to without even explaining what happened.'

'But he's not going anywhere now,' I said softly.

'How do you know that?' she asked.

I didn't. I suppose she was right. Trust had to be earned. I'd just been grateful that Raghu didn't have a girlfriend and hadn't really wanted to talk to him when he wanted to kiss me.

33

I woke up to a nightmare. I stepped out of my room, wondering where Raghu was. Nisha thought I needed to lay some ground rules and I wasn't sure how to go about it. Wouldn't it be presumptuous of me? Hadn't he said we should take it one day at a time? What was I to do?

When I walked into the living room, the atmosphere was tense.

Nani was sitting on the sofa, surrounded by three large suitcases, and glaring angrily at Aunty V. Aunty V looked solemn and Ma looked pale and was holding Papa's hand tightly. Papa's face was flushed and I could see he was restraining himself with great difficulty from saying something.

When had Nani come? What was going on?

Nani's eyes fell on me and she smiled. 'Come, come,' she said, patting the seat beside her.

Reluctantly, I sat next to her. The tableau remained stiff and frozen—there was just one more person in it!

Finally, Nani started talking in a hushed, important sounding voice, as if she was on the verge of breaking down. 'I kept waiting and waiting and waiting to see if she would call me, but my only daughter doesn't even want me to be there during the birth of my grandchild.'

Ma winced slightly. 'You were there during Ananya's birth. That was more than enough,' she snapped.

I sensed Nani stiffening beside me. She started speaking but her words were lost to me as I spotted Raghu walking in. He looked around mystified, but swiftly understood that it was tense.

'Ananya, breakfast?' he nodded towards the kitchen.

I nodded and got up gratefully.

Nani glared at Raghu too and her mouth tightened.

As Raghu and I reached the corridor that led to the kitchen, he held my hand. The gesture warmed my heart.

'That's your Nani, right?' he asked in a whisper.

I nodded. 'Yes, that's her. She's such a pain,' I whispered back.

'I got that vibe. How come you're dressed to go out?' he asked, looking at me up and down.

I flushed under his scrutiny. 'I was planning to meet Nisha,' I said.

He raised an eyebrow. 'To talk about us, I presume,' he said, rolling his eyes. He muttered 'girls' under his breath.

I was instantly annoyed. 'You presume wrong,' I said. 'Anirudh is also going to be there.'

'Yeah, big difference,' he said lightly, shaking his head. His face brightened suddenly. 'Shall I drop you off at Nisha's?' he asked.

'But how?' I asked, feeling pleased despite my uneasiness. Ground rules, Nisha's voice boomed in my head.

'Auto, how else? I'll drop you and go to the restaurant. This way I can spend some more time with you,' he explained, squeezing my hand gently.

His words made me very happy, but I was wary of showing it to him. I wanted to ask him the questions Nisha had raised last night but this wasn't the right place. Not with everyone outside.

Raghu started talking about something else. 'Hey, so I talked to my mother last night. I told her I wanted to do BHM, the hotel management degree course,' he said, still playing with my fingers.

'Oh, what did she say?'

'She was surprised and pleased and said we could definitely work on it,' he said, looking happy himself.

'And what about your father? Will he be okay with it?'

He shrugged. 'My mom will handle him,' he said. 'It's my future after all.'

I so badly wanted to ask him if I was a part of this future he was planning but the words got stuck in my mouth when he suddenly pushed me towards the wall, and stepped in front of me. My eyes widened.

'What are you doing?' I asked as he stepped closer.

'Kissing my girlfriend,' he said in a low voice, bending his head to kiss me.

Girlfriend! He said I was his girlfriend.

My entire face felt prickly. Making out with Raghu while our families were sitting in the next room was sheer madness, no matter how much I wanted it to go on.

I gulped and stepped away from him, hoping that no one would walk into the kitchen suddenly. I took an apple from the fridge and bit into it, hoping the random mundane activity would slow down my racing heart.

He frowned and turned me around, holding my shoulders like last night.

'Raghu, Nani's here. She's eagle-eyed,' I said.

He made a face. 'Is everything all right with you?' he asked.

'Yes, it is,' I assured him. But I couldn't meet his gaze and I stepped away from his hold.

I could hear raised voices. Papa, saying something and then Nani replying. If I was already feeling the beginning of a headache, I wondered how Ma was doing. Why was Nani fighting with them anyway?

I was glad Raghu didn't pursue his question as he picked up his phone and booked the auto.

'You don't want breakfast?' I asked him.

He shook his head. 'You?' he asked.

I showed him my apple. He nodded.

Nisha was right. There was so much we had to talk about. Why I was the way I was. What changes had happened to me in the five years we had stayed out of touch. I was sure he had changed too. We couldn't just kiss and pretend that everything was hunky dory. We could kiss, yes, but we had to talk too.

'Listen, can we talk? Later? Somewhere this drama isn't happening?' I asked him.

He frowned. 'Yeah, sure. What do you want to talk about?' he asked, picking up his backpack and slinging it over his shoulder.

I looked down. 'Maybe we could meet when you're free later today? When you finish up at the restaurant maybe?' I suggested.

His eyebrows went up. 'Um, you know I finish late. But we can meet up later today. I can always head out to meet you for a bit somewhere near the restaurant. But it will have to be in Indiranagar,' he said, moving towards the door.

'No problem. Tell me when you've got a spot of free time,' I said, following him.

He turned around and gave me one of his heart-stopping smiles. 'You just want to spend more time with me, right?' he said, raising an eyebrow.

I rolled my eyes but couldn't help but smile back at him.

'Whatever,' I said, even though I remembered Nisha's words. 'It's important,' I added.

He frowned but nodded. 'I'll text you when I'm free. We can go over to one of those dessert places on 12th Main,' he said. Dessert. Sheesh.

Ma's voice came to my ears loudly and clearly. 'There is no shame in having a baby at forty-three, Ma! This attitude is exactly why I didn't call you over.'

Nani's voice sounded placatory, though I could not hear the words. I felt anger rise towards her. She was shaming Ma for getting pregnant? How dare she? I was itching to go and tell off Nani, but Raghu took a hold of my wrist and firmly steered me towards the door.

He didn't let go even when the auto arrived. I finally shook my hand free from his to get inside and sat down in the corner, breathing heavily.

'Let it go. They'll be fine,' he said.

His words annoyed me suddenly. 'How will they be fine? Ma didn't want Nani to come over because she makes her angry like this,' I said. 'This is going to increase her blood pressure and . . . the baby is due any time now . . . ' I trailed off and looked out of the auto.

He held my hand. 'Hey, your dad is there and so is my mom. It's going to be all right.'

I didn't respond. Something low and intense crept over my belly as he moved closer to me, still holding my hand.

'What's changed since last night, Ananya?' he asked.

I looked at him then, his earnest eyes and perfect face — okay his face wasn't perfect, but it was to me. He smiled, but his eyes looked vulnerable.

I had seen that adoring yet worried look on his face before. Long ago. When he had first met Esha.

I didn't know how to answer him *now*. This had to be a part of the conversation we would have later.

'That I'm your girlfriend now?' I asked him instead, trying to keep my voice light and breezy.

He looked at me intently just as the auto jumped over a pothole, bringing him closer to me.

'I thought that part was obvious,' he said.

'I would rather have everything spelled out than assume anything in these matters,' I told him, something I was beginning to feel rather strongly.

'What matters?' he asked, raising an eyebrow.

I held his hand tightly and impulsively picked it up to kiss his knuckles. His bright smile warmed me. In matters of love, a voice in my head spoke. I didn't say anything.

34

When I got off the auto at Nisha's, Raghu carried on in the same auto to the restaurant. He waved as he left and I waved back at him, my mind a confused tangle of emotions. I exhaled, hoping that the talk with Nisha and Anirudh would help me figure things out in my head.

Anirudh was already there and the three of us sat down in her room to talk. Well, *they* were talking. I could barely concentrate. I was wondering what Nani was doing at home. Was she still at loggerheads with Ma? I had a sudden horrifying thought. Where was she going to sleep? Surely, she wasn't going to kick out Aunty V and Raghu from the guest room?

I texted Ma. 'Are you okay?' I asked her.

'Yes, why wouldn't I be?' she replied.

'Because of Nani.'

I hated it when people pretended everything was all right when they clearly weren't.

'Nothing to worry,' came the curt response.

'How long is she here for? Where's she going to sleep?' I typed out quickly.

There was no response from Ma. Annoyed, I kept looking at my phone, waiting for it to ping.

Nisha looked at me and smiled. 'Didn't he just drop you here? Waiting for a text from him?' she asked.

I shook my head as my phone pinged.

Ma: 'She'll sleep with V in the guest room.'

My heart sank. What about Raghu?

Another text filled the screen. 'I've asked Raghu if he can sleep in the living room for a few days on the sofa. He says it's okay.'

I put my phone away. It was a relief to know that Raghu wasn't going anywhere yet. He was bound to return to Mumbai once his apprenticeship ended, even if Aunty V stayed for Ma's delivery. What would happen to us when he left?

'What's going on?' Nisha nudged me.

I told them about Nani's surprise visit and the texts from Ma.

'So now your house is full!' Nisha remarked.

I nodded. 'I just hope it won't make things worse. I'm worried for Ma. She just doesn't get along with Nani.'

'And what's going on with you and Raghu?' she asked.

I tried to compose my thoughts. I was sure she had told Anirudh everything by now, but it felt odd to discuss my love life with the two of them. For the first time ever.

'I'm confused,' I admitted finally.

'About what you feel?' she asked.

I shook my head. 'That part is probably the least confusing,' I told her with a grim smile. 'I've always liked him. I've always felt happy to have him around. When we were kids, it was just because he was so much fun to be with.'

'And now?' Nisha persisted.

I took a deep breath. 'Now, I like him a lot. I think . . . I think I'm in love with him,' I said, choking out the words.

Nisha looked at me with wide eyes and Anirudh coughed slightly.

'Er, wow. From not being able to stand him to this . . .' Nisha trailed off.

I shrugged. 'I think my anger with him all these years stemmed from my feelings for him,' I rationalized. 'Listen, I agree with what you said and I've asked to meet him later today, outside the house so we can talk without all the distractions. I'll bring up all the things you mentioned.'

Anirudh's eyebrows went up. 'What things?' he asked. I shrugged.

'About the need for us to communicate . . . about how he can't take me for granted because we've been friends for so long. And also . . .'

'Also?' Nisha asked curiously.

'Also about my body issues. He needs to know that, and he needs to know how hard I've worked to reach where I am. I haven't told you guys but his mother keeps sending me these body neutrality links . . .'

'Body what?' Nisha asked, eyes wide.

I told them whatever I'd read and been thinking about. Their expressions weren't saying much.

'What?' I asked finally.

Anirudh looked uncomfortable but he nodded somewhat encouragingly. 'I feel like this is what Nisha and I have been trying to tell you all along,' he said finally.

'Yeah, and it's taken you so long to get your head around it. We didn't know it was called body-neutrality or that there's a whole movement or whatever. We don't know the labels. But we do know that you're awesome and it's to do with you. As a person. Not what you look like, and especially not what your body looks like,' Nisha said. She looked nervous as she said it.

She turned to Anirudh for support and I caught that fleeting look on his face, that easily readable look which proclaimed to everyone that he loved her. It was fascinating the way his expression changed when she directed her gaze at him. Was my face as transparent as his? Had Nisha seen and understood what his expression meant?

'Ananya, we know you've been to a lot of trouble to change how you look. We're not saying that was pointless. But there's a reason you have to stop hating your body. And, like what this movement says, you don't have to love your body either. Just think of your body as *a* body,' she said.

'So I don't have to think about how fat and ugly and disgusting I am,' I asked, relishing the words even as they pierced my heart.

Nisha held my hand firmly and shook her head. She looked livid. 'You are not any of those things.'

'You're my friend. You're going to say that anyway. I don't have any special qualities,' I told her.

She frowned. 'What?'

'I'm mediocre in every way. Looks, studies and of course, that elusive thing that I need to figure out about my future,' I said.

'That's because you're normal. Like me,' she said.

I snorted. 'We're hardly anything alike,' I told her in an accusatory tone.

She narrowed her eyes. 'Because I know what I want to do? I'll be studying architecture, but there's no guarantee I'll stick to just being an architect later on in life. Or is it because I'm thin and you're not? Dude, we're all human. We're *all* imperfect. My arms are like sticks and I wish they weren't like that but I don't hate myself. I'm okay with it,' she insisted.

It wasn't really the same, I thought. Thin people weren't shamed the same way fat people were. All the same, I listened to her in silence, wishing she'd said this to me earlier, when I'd waged a battle against my body. She had tried — but I hadn't taken her seriously.

I was so quiet that I could sense their uneasiness. Both Nisha and Anirudh were watching me silently.

She leant forward and hugged me quickly. 'You're one of the most awesome people I know. There's nothing ugly about you. Not now. Not ever. I really need you to start believing that,' she said.

'I know . . .'

'Your awesomeness has nothing to do with how much you weighed or weigh,' she said fiercely.

I hugged her again. Sometimes words weren't enough to convey feelings.

35

I stayed at Nisha's for a little while longer, not willing to go back home to face Nani and her intrusive questions.

Anirudh accompanied me to the door. He was leaving too. They both were frantically preparing for their various entrance exams and had taken out some time for me.

'Shall I drop you off at home?' he asked with a smile. He picked up his helmet from near the door and looked at me with his eyebrows raised.

'Okay,' I told him. His Scooty was parked near the gate. He removed an extra helmet from below the seat and handed it to me.

'Thanks,' I muttered as I strapped it on my head. My house wasn't too far away, but Anirudh was always cautious about everything. If I told him that there were no cops around and we wouldn't be caught if both of us weren't wearing helmets, he would most likely be very confused. Because he was one of the few people who wore a helmet for safety and not because he didn't want to get caught by the police.

A part of me wanted to ask him how he knew that Nisha was more than a friend. How had he known about his feelings for her? Because that could help me understand Raghu's attraction to me. I didn't ask him because it was silly. Raghu and Anirudh were two very different guys. I couldn't generalize their feelings like that.

As Anirudh dropped me off, I spotted Nani sitting on the wicker chair on the porch and glaring at me. I kept my face impassive as I walked inside.

When would Raghu call me? I wanted to go meet him right away but since it was lunchtime, he wouldn't even have the time to text me. I really wanted to meet him, and talk about everything, get it over with so we could move on with our lives.

Things at home seemed okay on the surface. Ma was lying in her room, sleeping peacefully when I looked in on her. Nani ambled back inside but I didn't want to be caught alone with her so I rushed off to my room, claiming I had a headache. I kept looking at my phone, willing it to buzz so I could go and meet Raghu.

When I emerged from my room to get something to eat, Aunty V and Nani seemed to have come to a truce of sorts because they were both cooking away.

Nani beckoned me closer. 'Who was that boy who dropped you off?' she asked.

'My friend Anirudh,' I said.

She didn't interrogate me further but asked if I wanted to have lunch. She was frying popcorn chicken in a kadai. I backed away with a tight smile.

'Want some of this?' Aunty V asked.

The bowl of salad looked so much nicer than the salads I normally made for myself. It had orange segments and walnuts, greens, pear slices and just a drizzle of a honey-lemon dressing. I piled some on a plate and caught the gloating look Aunty V shot in Nani's direction.

Nani huffed and turned away. Rolling my eyes, I thought that if Ma's BP wasn't hanging in balance, all this would have been damn funny.

I took my plate to Ma's room. She was just waking up.

'What's that?' she asked, wrinkling her nose in disgust.

'Some really delicious salad Aunty V made. I'm actually thinking of going for seconds.' I let the words slip before I realized what I'd said. I hadn't had seconds in a very long time.

Ma looked impressed. 'Are you doing all right?' she asked as she pushed her hair behind and tied it in a haphazard bun. She looked tired and pale and there were dark circles under her eyes which accentuated how listless she looked. She winced as the baby kicked. I frowned when I saw her belly actually move up and then go down a little. Wow. Major shivers.

'I'm all right, but how long is Nani going to be here?'

'Till the delivery,' Ma said grimly. 'I'm going to need all hands on deck, especially you, Ananya.'

I nodded.

'If there's any tension between Nani and V, you have to defuse it,' she said.

How did she expect me to do that?

'I don't want your Nani chasing off V and Raghu. They're very important to me, especially at this time,' Ma said.

I felt my face flush idiotically the moment Ma mentioned Raghu's name.

'For me too,' I told her.

'I'm hungry. Is lunch ready?' she asked.

I nodded. I wondered if there was going to be a war over food in my house. Just what I needed, I thought as both Aunty V and Nani called out to Ma to come and eat.

I went to the kitchen and served myself some more of the salad when my phone buzzed. It was a message from Raghu.

'Meet me in two hours?'

He hadn't specified where he wanted to meet me, so I decided to surprise him in the restaurant.

'But why?' Ma asked when I told her I was heading out to meet Raghu about an hour later. I'd met Nisha

and Anirudh this morning so it was best that I stuck
to the truth.

Ma was sitting in the living room, watching TV.
Lunch had been a chaotic affair with both Aunty V and
Nani trying to force Ma to eat what they had cooked.

'He wanted to discuss something,' I said as
I tightened the laces on my sneakers. I snuck out before
Nani could give me knowing looks or the third degree.

When my auto reached the restaurant where Raghu
was interning, I looked around nervously. It was a
single-storied structure that looked like a bungalow in
a posh lane.

There was a young man outside, standing at a
desk, guiding people and checking their reservations.
There were not too many people as lunchtime was
nearly over.

I tried to march inside but he stopped me. 'Lunch
hours are over,' he informed me.

I felt my face flush. ' I'm here to meet Raghu,'
I said.

He frowned.

'He works in the kitchen,' I added quickly.

Understanding dawned. 'If he's in the kitchen,
he won't be free for another half hour at least,' the
man said.

Shit. I was really early. I could text him and tell
him I was here already but I didn't want to hurry him
up. Let him finish whatever it was he had to do.

'Can I wait for him inside, please?' I asked.

The man hesitated, but then nodded.

The darkened interiors of the restaurant smelt so good. The many different aromas floating around here clawed at my stomach. I found a low settee to sit on near the entrance.

Most of the people were finishing and leaving. I pulled out my phone and played a game.

One of the waiters asked me courteously if he could help me. He was tall and well-built and quite cute even though he didn't seem much older than Raghu.

I looked up at him self-consciously. 'I . . . um, I'm here for Raghu.'

'I'll tell him you're here,' he said and wandered off to a door at the end of the corridor to one side.

Because the restaurant was nearly empty and quiet, and the volume of the music had been lowered, I heard him loud and clear as he called out:

'Raghu, some fat chick's here to meet you.'

36

I was twelve all over again.

I sat frozen on that settee for the barest of moments and then I sprang up. My heart was pounding painfully as I walked towards the door.

I heard Raghu call out my name and I turned around. The waiter I had spoken to sauntered out after him, smirking.

Maybe it was because of the look on his face, I decided not to run away. I was going to stand my ground, I thought, and glared at him.

'Hey! I thought we weren't meeting for another half an hour?' Raghu said, a little anxiously.

The waiter came up and put an arm around Raghu's shoulder.

Raghu pulled it off irritably. 'Aamir, please apologize to my friend,' he said, turning to him. 'You were really rude.'

Aamir just rolled his eyes.

So I was his friend now. Not girlfriend. Something inside me didn't want to let it go because if he was embarrassed by me, I wanted to embarrass him further.

'Actually,' I said smiling up sweetly to this Aamir, 'as of last night, I'm his girlfriend.'

Aamir raised his eyebrows as though in appreciation, but I knew he was mocking me.

Raghu did look embarrassed at that.

'It's very easy to call someone fat, like it's an insult,' I said.

Raghu's eyes narrowed and he opened his mouth to intervene, but I didn't let him. Aamir still had that insufferable smile on his face.

'It's taken a lot of hard work and many years for me to not think of myself as worthless just because I'm fat. There's more to me than my body weight,' I told him, remembering Nisha's words, the many articles I'd read over the past few days that Aunty V had shared with me. 'And if you think you're going to make me feel ashamed about my weight, you're wrong.'

I turned around and walked to the door, not really caring if Raghu was following me because after making such a statement, it was best to walk away, head held high. I was quivering with rage but glad that I hadn't run away as I'd wanted to at first. When I reached the bright sunlight outside, I felt thankful.

Only then did I feel Raghu's presence behind me.

'Come,' he said.

We walked together, not really sure of where we were going. The road was full of places where we could sit and eat.

I was high on adrenaline and I wanted to inhale an entire brownie if I could. For the first time in years, I remembered those triple chocolate brownies that I'd made for that bitch Esha. I wished I had tasted at least one before wasting them on her.

I saw the brightly coloured façade of one of those cafés that specialized in desserts in front of me and didn't think twice before walking inside. Delicious smells of toasty shortbread, coffee and chocolate accosted me.

I turned to Raghu, right behind me, who was looking around. His gaze finally landed on mine and he didn't look away.

But I was angry with him and so I glared back. His gaze softened and he touched my cheek lightly.

I shook my head. 'Let's find a place to sit,' I told him tightly.

We found a table against a wall. Even though it was past three in the afternoon, there were lots of people here. I sat down and avoided looking at Raghu for a bit, looking around and taking in the surroundings.

'Ananya,' he began but I cut him off with a wave of my hand.

'Are you embarrassed of me?' I asked him. My cheeks felt hot even as I asked the words.

'I'm not,' he said, shaking his head vehemently. 'I was just embarrassed at having *a* girlfriend because then I'd always be teased about it and I prefer to just do my thing and not get into all that.' He looked earnest. Always so focused on his work, I thought, marvelling at how much he had changed since we were kids.

I decided to come right out and ask him what I wanted to know.

'Why did you go back to Mumbai without telling me?' I asked him.

He looked up and then he leaned forward. 'I think we should get something so they don't kick us out,' he whispered.

Grimly, I nodded.

'What do you want?' he asked.

We were surrounded by desserts. Oh god. Sweets and desserts had been my undoing. I couldn't go down that path again. But the five years that I'd avoided them had been so joyless. Did I have to live that way all my life and *still* look fat? I might as well give in a little and enjoy life, and then worry about burning off the calories.

'Get that raspberry parfait with the white chocolate brownie,' I told him, pointing to the dessert slideshow on the flat screen TV. As Raghu walked to the counter to place the order, I looked around and spotted myself in a mirror on the opposite wall.

I looked away quickly, but then, I forced myself to look back into the mirror. The voices didn't begin their insidious whispering because Fat Ananya was still there, smiling shyly at me. She was part of me. She *was* me.

Around me, there was just the noise of the busy café, the music playing on the sound system, the laughter of a group of boys and girls—nothing to indicate that I'd just had an epiphany.

Raghu returned and sat down opposite me.

'You didn't answer my question,' I said.

He looked down at the table. 'I'm sorry. I didn't think it was a big deal at that time,' he said softly.

'What? You went away without talking to me after that . . .'

'Hospital moment,' he added, his face a little pink.

'How can you say that it wasn't a big deal? And when you returned to Mumbai, you just ignored me. Didn't send me a single message until I sent you that selfie with my friends,' I said.

'Ananya, I'm sorry. I was confused.' He looked around and then reached out to take my hand.

'When I came to Bangalore, I was looking forward to catching up with you, even though you'd given me the cold shoulder all these years. But then . . . you were still mad at me and then, after we talked and got Esha out of the way, I started to feel something for you, every time I saw you.'

I leaned forward, my hand suddenly feeling warm in his.

'I couldn't believe the thoughts I was having, how I kept thinking of you all the time, how I wanted to spend more and more time with you. And on the day of the party, you looked so different and that's when I realized that I had a crush on you,' he said.

My mouth dropped open and my ears turned hot. He looked sheepish as he turned my hand over in his. 'And I ran away back to Mumbai to figure out everything. And anyway, my dad had been after me to take those exams.'

'That's not really an excuse for ignoring me,' I murmured.

He nodded. 'I know. I was a coward. I hated being back in Mumbai and then you sent me that selfie and I wanted to come back to Bangalore right away. And then, once we were back to texting, it just felt right. Our communication seemed so fluid, so easy. And when I came to your house last night from the airport, seeing you in person just brought everything back in a rush. All my feelings. Everything.'

I looked away, trying to compose myself. Raghu was still talking.

'I'm so glad you gave it back to that dickhead Aamir. What an ass,' he said, shaking his head.

'He was rude, but he spoke the truth. I'm fat. Less than I used to be but I am still overweight. I don't know if it will ever go away. I'm just going to have to live with it,' I said with finality.

The server brought our dessert to the table.

Raghu pulled his chair towards my side of the table and sat down beside me.

'I don't care about that as long as you're okay,' he said.

Smiling, I put my head on his shoulder.

'This is going to melt if we don't eat it soon,' Raghu said after some time.

I straightened up, feeling self-conscious suddenly, and picked up a spoon. As I pushed my spoon into the dessert, I sensed Raghu coming nearer, and I felt heat bloom over my skin because of his proximity.

I caught a group of girls looking at us. One or two of them giggled and raised their eyebrows appreciatively in Raghu's direction. They were probably wondering what a hottie like him was doing with me.

Too bad I wasn't up to explaining anything to anyone!

I smiled at them sweetly and brought the laden spoon, not to my mouth but to Raghu's. He looked surprised but he smiled as he leaned forward to close his mouth around the spoon.

And then, he did the same for me.

The cold dessert slid into my stomach and churned uneasily. I tried to not count the calories I was consuming or think of the amount of exercise I would have to do to get rid of the fat that would end up on my thighs.

When we were finished, Raghu had this strange heated look in his eyes that made me blush.

I wanted to stay here longer, talking to him freely without worrying about being overheard. But I also knew that it was time to go. Ma would be wondering what I was doing and with Nani at home, one never knew what to expect.

'Do you have to go back to the restaurant?' I asked him. He nodded. I hadn't even left and I was already missing him.

'I'll see you tonight,' he said as we walked outside the café. The afternoon was warm and I was happy.

'I can't wait,' I blurted out and his face broke into a smile.

'Come here,' he said in that low voice which did all sorts of things to me.

I shook my head and stepped back. 'Not here.'

'Um, I wasn't planning on doing anything,' he said, looking all too innocent as he stepped near me.

'Yeah, right. I know that grin on your face.'

'I swear no one is even going to notice,' he insisted as he drew me closer to him.

'I'd rather have you kiss me somewhere where *I'll* notice it,' I said to him and that stopped him in his tracks. I grinned at the expression on his face.

'Fine. Your house. The garden. Tonight. Don't give me excuses about your Nani,' he bit out.

'I won't,' I told him and touched his cheek lightly. His gaze softened as he kissed the tips of my fingers.

37

Ma looked at me strangely when I walked back into the house. I wondered if she could read my face. She and Nani were both reading in the living room, Ma on her Kindle and Nani some magazine.

Nani frowned. 'Where were you?' she asked me.

'Out,' I replied, hoping she wouldn't persist.

'Out where?' she insisted.

I took a deep breath.

'She had gone to meet Raghu,' Ma said suddenly.

I looked at her surprised. I had not expected her to speak for me.

'I don't like this, boys and girls meeting alone,' Nani said, still frowning.

My face flushed. I went to my room and I could hear Ma and Nani arguing behind me.

I wondered if Raghu would feel unsettled because he didn't have a room for himself now. His things were still in the guest room but he couldn't just go there if he wanted to. His other refuge, the kitchen, had been appropriated by Nani.

I stayed in my room and came out only in the evening. Raghu had texted that he would be home a little early today and I was counting the minutes.

When he walked in, we were all sitting stiffly in the living room, waiting for Papa to get back from work so that we could have dinner. Nani became more alert the moment Raghu's eyes met mine. I couldn't control the blush that crept into my cheeks. I looked away—straight into Nani's narrowed eyes.

When Raghu rejoined us after a shower, I couldn't stop myself from looking at him every now and then. I tried to be surreptitious but he was stealing glances at me as well. Nani fumed silently.

Ma had told me that Nani had hated Papa on sight. She could not understand why Ma would want to marry him because Papa didn't have much money. But Ma had persisted and well, Papa hadn't turned out too bad, I thought. Maybe that annoyed Nani. But shouldn't she be happy that her daughter was happy and doing well?

Nani had never liked Aunty V either, and now because Ma had called her in preference to Nani, she probably hated her.

As Nani got up to check on the dinner that she had insisted on cooking, we heard Papa's car at the gate.

When Papa came in and saw our glum faces, his too became glum. It was like a reflection, I thought, trying not to giggle.

'She's still here then,' he said in a low voice as he sat down.

'Of course she's still here,' Aunty V said. 'Making a number of heart-attack friendly dishes.'

'Mom!' Raghu mumbled. 'Stop it.'

Aunty V rolled her eyes, but it was Ma who spoke. 'Just let her be. Let her do what she wants. She'll get tired of it in a few days.'

Dinner was a strained affair. I ended up sitting next to Raghu and Nani glowered at the two of us.

Nani had made lacchha parathas and rogan josh. There was an inch-thick layer of oil on the gravy. Just looking at it made me want to hurl. I quickly made myself a cucumber and carrot salad.

To my surprise, Nani smiled approvingly.

'See, Ananya, I've told you so many times that no one likes fat girls. So it's good that you are doing some dieting. Otherwise, if you are not careful, you will become a saand like your father and you may not be as lucky as he was, to get someone beautiful like my Chitra. Of course, I can't say *she* was very lucky when she got married to him. But I can see that you are doing something about your weight,' she said with a smile that was meant to be approving.

Raghu's hand tightened over mine as my ears buzzed. Everyone looked either horrified or shocked at how Nani had managed to insult the entire family in one monologue.

'You can't speak to my family like that!' Ma said, her face flushing in a way that worried me. Ma shouldn't be getting so angry. It wasn't good for her or the baby!

'I didn't say anything that wasn't true,' Nani defended herself.

'Ma, please calm down,' I told her. But she looked like a volcano that was about to erupt.

Suddenly, Ma clutched her stomach and winced, her face screwing up in pain. 'Something is happening!' she gasped.

'What?' I shouted. Everyone got up all at once.

'Shekhar, she needs to go to the hospital!' Aunty V said as Ma bent over double, breathing through her mouth.

In a series of uncoordinated and haphazard moves, we managed to get Ma to the car. Aunty V picked up the bag that Ma had packed some days back, and Papa ordered Nani to calm down and to get inside the car with Ma.

The baby was coming!

38

There wasn't any space for Raghu so he said he would follow us in an auto. Papa started the car. Nani and Aunty V were in the back, trying to help Ma breathe. I was in front, on the phone with the doctor, not knowing anything that the doctor was asking me. How was it possible for water to break? Because that was what the doctor kept asking.

I asked Ma anyway, and she shook her head. The doctor said she would come to the hospital soon.

The journey seemed interminable and I kept turning around to look at Ma's flushed face.

As soon as we reached, nurses whisked Ma away. This was it! Despite my fears, I was excited.

Raghu joined us soon and we all waited until Ma was shifted to the labour ward. The gynaecologist came to check in on Ma and then came outside to call Papa to one side. Papa's face paled.

Something was wrong. No! My heart raced and I felt like throwing up. Was something wrong with Ma? Or the baby?

Papa came back speak to Aunty V and Nani in low tones.

Nani looked annoyed. 'But why does she want to operate? There is still time, no?'

Papa shot an angry look at her and said something, which again I couldn't hear. And then he said, 'I'm giving them the consent for surgery.' He went off.

'What's going to happen?' I asked Aunty V.

She shook her head and tried to smile.

'Nothing to worry. The doctor has decided to go with surgery because the baby is in distress,' she said, patting my arm.

'What? How is that nothing to worry?' I asked her, trying not to screech. *The baby is in distress.* What did that mean?

Aunty V shook her head. 'Really, she and the baby will be fine.' But her eyes looked worried.

Raghu came up beside me and I caught his hand, needing comfort. I didn't care if Aunty V or Nani saw that.

Ma was wheeled to the operation theatre on the third floor. Ma's face looked bloated and she was in obvious pain. We followed her until she was taken inside.

We waited outside in silence. I was still holding Raghu's hand, near the door. Papa paced, rubbing his forehead every now and then. Nani and Aunty V sat on some plastic chairs.

'I'm so scared,' I whispered.

'I'm scared too,' he admitted. I was glad he wasn't giving any platitudes about how it was all going to be fine.

Nani gave me a dirty look, and her eyes shifted to our clasped hands.

I glared back at her. My little brother or sister was in distress *because* of her. She had made Ma angry.

I was reminded of countless Hindi movies I'd seen where people waited outside the operation theatre, for a doctor to come and give them news. This was not like the night we had spent in the hospital a few months ago. Because things were different then. Now, something was imminent.

The doctor stepped out just when I felt I could not bear it any longer. She smiled warmly and said, 'Congratulations! It's a boy!'

We broke into cheers. Papa's first question was 'How's Chitra?'

'She's fine. We couldn't give her full anaesthesia so she's awake. You can see her in some time,' the doctor assured us. 'It's a good thing we did this right away.'

I asked, 'And the baby? Is he fine?'

The doctor nodded. 'The baby is fine. You can see him in a bit but we'll keep him in the incubator tonight,' she said.

The exhilaration I felt was so keen that I wanted to run around screaming with joy. All our worried faces now shone with happiness. Ma and the baby were both fine!

Some time later, a nurse called us. One by one, we were allowed to go up closer to the incubator in the nursery and see him.

He was pink and scrawny and had a shock of black hair. He was beautiful. I was overcome with emotion. Little twit. I couldn't imagine I'd hated him when I'd first heard that Ma was pregnant.

Papa's eyes were wet and shiny.

Ma was in pain when we saw her, but so relieved and happy—and so were we. Everything was fine. Everything was good.

Nani tried to ruin the moment by saying, *thank goodness, finally, it was a boy.* But Papa asked Nani to step out with him for a bit. I don't know what he said, but Nani kept her mouth shut for the rest of the visit.

Since only one person could stay back at the hospital, Ma said she wanted Aunty V and insisted the rest of us go back home.

Papa, Nani, Raghu and I were quiet on the way back home. Nani went off immediately to the guest room to sleep. Wordlessly, Raghu and I set about cleaning the remnants of our disastrous dinner. I was exhausted and exhilarated at the same time. It was like an adrenaline high.

Papa came in in his pajamas and looked at us sheepishly. 'I'm still hungry,' he said.

'We *just* packed away everything,' I told him, annoyed.

'Not a problem, Uncle. I can heat up the parathas and the gravy for you,' Raghu offered.

I narrowed my eyes. He was clearly trying to get into my father's good books. The thought amused and warmed me at the same time.

'I have a better idea. Have this instead,' I said, offering Papa the salad I had been eating. The expression on his face was priceless. 'Let Raghu go to sleep. He's tired,' I said firmly.

'No, I'm fine,' Raghu insisted, but I shook my head.

Papa took the salad bowl and went away, muttering to himself.

Raghu and I were alone in the kitchen, as we had been countless other times these past few months. But this was different. He knew it and I knew it. But he didn't make a move, probably because he was worried Papa would stroll back any moment.

'You don't have to butter up Papa, you know,' I said softly.

Raghu glanced at me quickly, a little surprised. 'Um, I wasn't . . . err . . .' he trailed off.

I cocked my head slightly. 'Really? You would have heated everything and served it to him if I wasn't your girlfriend?' I asked.

'Of course,' he said. 'It's not like I was trying to impress Uncle.'

'Really?' I insisted, my arms crossed and he finally grinned.

'Okay, okay, you're right,' he admitted. 'But even if you weren't my girlfriend, I'd have done it. Because I'd be hoping to make a good impression on you.' His eyes glittered as he said that.

'I was thinking of sitting outside in the garden for a bit,' I said pointedly.

He raised an eyebrow. 'At *this* time of the night, Ananya? *Whatever* will your Nani say?' he said softly as he prowled towards me, trying to trap me in front of the counter.

'I think we should find out for ourselves,' I told him as I ducked and escaped, laughing.

'She's most likely going to join us, considering all this noise you're making,' he muttered as he switched off the kitchen light and followed me outside through the back door.

It was a quiet night. We couldn't see a single star in the sky but then, we weren't really looking. Raghu didn't even wait till we reached the garden. He whirled me around and had me in his arms the moment I stepped outside and then we were kissing.

Epilogue

None of us had slept in days. Weeks. Months. Even years.

Okay, that was an exaggeration but that's how it *felt*.

My little terror of a brother, Arjun, ensured that no one got a decent night's sleep once we brought him and Ma back from the hospital. He didn't cry. He screamed. And we all rushed around and fell over one another to see how we could make things better for the little emperor.

After a week, Nani decided she was going back to Chandigarh. No one knew what Papa said to her at the hospital.

When Arjun was a month old, Aunty V said it was time for her to go back to Mumbai. We were all sitting in the living room, and Ma was rocking Arjun to sleep in her arms. I looked at Raghu in dismay.

But Aunty V announced that Raghu had been accepted at a hotel management college in Bangalore and would be staying at the hostel. I looked at him in delighted surprise.

Why didn't you tell me?

I texted though he was sitting right there. He looked at his phone and smiled.

Because I wanted it to be a surprise.

I smiled back, unable to contain my happiness.

Ma put Arjun down in the crib and looked over at both of us.

'What about your girlfriend, Raghu?' she asked him sweetly.

I looked away, pretending to be busy unfolding and refolding Arjun's clothes on the sofa. Ma was no fool.

'Um . . . I . . . she . . .' Raghu stammered.

'What girlfriend?' Aunty V intervened, frowning. 'Why didn't you tell me about her? Who's she? Is she in Mumbai? Didn't I ask you if you wanted to join a college in Mumbai or even Pune but *you* wanted to join here in Bangalore.'

My heart did another happy dance.

'Mom, we'll talk about this later,' Raghu said, his teeth gritted.

I was surprised that Aunty V hadn't caught on to what was happening between us, but Ma had. Ma looked at both of us fondly though and I looked away.

We heard Papa shut the gates, which made a loud screeching noise. Arjun woke up, startled. Ma looked tired and I told her, I'd take care of him for some time.

I picked up my baby brother, feeling my heart flood with love. And annoyance. He was going to be a major pain when he grew up. It helped that he was cute, though. Rocking him gently, I took him towards the dining room.

Raghu came and stood beside me. The two of us had been very discreet for the past month. We barely had time for stolen kisses, but now that Raghu was going to study in Bangalore, I felt like we had all the time in the world. Hopefully.

Andaleeb Wajid is the author of twenty-seven published novels and writes across different genres. Her horror novel *It Waits* was shortlisted for the MAMI Word to Screen 2017 and her series for teens, The Tamanna Trilogy has been optioned for screen by a reputed production house. Andaleeb's novel *When She Went Away* was shortlisted for The Hindu Young World Goodbooks Award in 2017.

Read more by Andaleeb Wajid

when she went away

Andaleeb Wajid

duckbill